# GHOSTED

## KAT ADDAMS

# CHAPTER ONE

CLAIRE

"Here. Take it." My mother grunted, heaving a dusty box labeled *Mischief* on top of the hood of her station wagon.

She'd had that wagon since my high school days when I would make her pull around to the back of the school to let me out. I wasn't embarrassed by the station wagon, though I'd let her believe that. It was my mother that I hid from my life.

"Thanks." I tugged at the box, prying it open and peering inside.

"Don't go opening that hocus-pocus around me!" She lit her cigarette, exhaling a cloud of smoke in one long-drawn-out sigh. "I've got enough demons in my life." She waved the smoke away from her face.

"So, you're saying you really believe Great Aunt Karen was a witch? Like a real witch?" I shut the box.

I didn't want to give my mom anything else to complain about. Already, since I'd been in town, I'd been listening to her woeful tales of irate coworkers, family I'd never met, and

1

a stupid gopher that she swore was after her. She'd told me that, a few weeks back, she grabbed a shovel and stepped out onto her porch, ready to hunt down the varmint making a mess of her lawn. But the moment she stepped off the porch, he barreled toward her in a tunnel of vengeance. She screamed, dropped her shovel, and ran back inside. Of course, I didn't believe her story. My mom had probably imagined the entire fiasco while she was on another one of her benders. She was a functioning alcoholic. That was what my therapist had labeled her.

"I believe that your great aunt was a quack! Maybe she's the gopher. Reincarnated to come back and try to get me out of her house. You have no idea the weird shit that happens in that house. It's a house though. And I don't have the money to move. Nothing's harmed me yet. Not even that damn rodent."

She pinched the bridge of her nose before wiping a bead of sweat off of her top lip and smearing her flaky rosy lipstick across her mouth. I knew by the way her hands began to shake that she'd need alcohol soon.

"I doubt she's the beaver, Mom." I glanced around the hotel parking lot, wondering if anyone was eavesdropping on our crazy conversation.

"Gopher. Not a beaver. And if you end up in the loony bin after opening that box, I'll say I told you so. I warned ya. But you've never been one to listen to your mom." She stubbed her cigarette out on the side of her car and flicked it on the curb.

I thought about responding that if I ended up in the loony bin, it would be from her parenting fails rather than a haunted box. But instead, I did what I always did. I nodded, accepted my fate, and kept my mouth shut—like a good daughter.

"I'll let you know if I have any questions. I'd better get

back to my room and start on this box. Boss lady wants my article finished by Halloween." I circled my arms around the heavy box and lifted, chipping off bits of rust from the station wagon that clung to the bottom.

"Why would *Choose Forks* blog want anything to do with Morningwood anyway?" she asked.

"Morningwood was recently named one of the most haunted places in America. Forks residents take day trips out here to see that kind of stuff, I guess. I don't know. All I know is that I have to nail this article or else I'm in trouble. I might need to stop by your house to look in the attic and make sure I'm not missing anything. I'll let you know."

"I'm sure there's a lot more up there. I grabbed the first box I saw and skedaddled out of there. Had an uneasy feeling from that attic. Your aunt probably cursed it or something." She shook her head. "But you can stop by my house anytime and take a look, dear. Just call first. You know … in case I'm napping." She pried open the car door with a shaky hand before settling into her seat. She tossed the seat-belt buckle to the side before turning her key in the ignition.

"I know you like your naps." I bit my tongue—again.

I'd walked into my mom's house while she was lying passed out, naked, and drunk more than enough times to scar me for life. These days, I opted for a hotel room instead of more therapy sessions to rid myself of those vivid memories seared into my brain.

"Toodaloo!" she said, rolling down her window and waving. She hacked, coughing her way out of the parking lot until I could no longer see or hear her.

I carried the heavy box past the hotel staff's curious gaze. There was nothing like small-town gossip. Already, I'd heard whispers echoing in the corridor about Annie Jackson's daughter—me. When I'd moved away from this place years ago, the entire town had taken it personally.

Nothing offended Morningwood folk like someone deciding life was better elsewhere. Outsiders passing through were tolerated. Newcomers were celebrated. But the people who left this hellhole for good would forever earn a stain on their local reputation. We weren't welcome here anymore. If you left, they didn't want you to come back. Ever. Hence the gossip, eye rolls, and the lack of cleaning service in my dusty, old hotel room. I'd been here for two days, and I still couldn't get a fresh towel.

I set the box down outside of my door and fished a metal key from my pocket. The Creaky Spring Inn was so old that the owner hadn't bothered to change the locks to digital keys yet. I pushed the door open and shoved the box inside with my foot, too exhausted to pick it up again. A cold blast of stale air rattled through the window air-conditioning unit, which I had tried to turn off several times already. It was no use. Even the maintenance man, Roger, couldn't fix it. He'd pried it open, jiggled a few nuts and bolts, and put it back together, shrugging his shoulders. I'd been sleeping under the blankets, layering those not-so-fresh towels over me for extra warmth.

"All right, Karen, let's see what you got for me." I rubbed my hands together and opened the box.

I piled old, tattered letters and melted candles on the side of the bed before reaching in and pulling out a locked jeweled box. I ran my hand along the top, accidentally knocking off one of the gaudy gemstones. I peered back into the cardboard box and grabbed a skeleton key that surely had to fit the lock.

"Probably contains the hair of a rat or eye of a newt," I said to myself.

I fumbled with the key, wiggling it into the rusted lock. To my astonishment—or good luck—the lock opened. A quick burst of light washed over the room, blinding me for a split second. I rubbed my eyes, looking toward the window for signs of lightning or a summer storm. But the sun shone brightly as ever outside. I shrugged my shoulders, told myself that I was delusional from the lack of sleep, and opened the box.

"Jeez," I said, staring down at a big blue dildo. "What the hell?"

I grabbed it, turning it in my palm. It twitched in my hand.

I screamed and threw it back into the box. "Magic dildo?"

I rummaged through the rest of the junk, pulling out odds and ends and separating them into piles, but my attention kept coming back to the haunted dildo. It had been a while since I'd played with a man or a toy. The last man I'd let in my bedroom left me for someone else, and my toys were as worn out as I was. Sex had been the last thing on my mind these last few months anyway. My sexual appetite had left with my ex.

*But now ...*

I glanced back over at the dildo before picking it up and carrying it to the sink. I wasn't taking any chances of getting dirty with something out of a witch's vagina. I scrubbed the plastic pecker under scalding water. It flinched in my hand.

*That can't be right.*

I paused, second-guessing if my horniness was worth this possible evil spell. I could lie back and spread my legs, and this thing could spearhead me into the headboard. There was no telling what type of curse my aunt had put on it. She'd always had a mean streak in her.

The dildo flexed in my palm. I quickly finished cleaning it and carried it straight to bed.

*Yep, worth it. Once-in-a-lifetime masturbation session with a cursed dick.*

I stripped off my clothes and slipped us both under the

blanket, giggling like a schoolgirl. Whatever spells had come out of that box, one must have gotten ahold of me too. I never giggled like a schoolgirl, much less stopped my work to fiddle my diddle.

I clutched the toy, rubbing it between my legs and up and over my clit. It softened, wiggling out of my hand.

I screamed, lifting the covers to see what was going on underneath. The big blue dildo took on the shape of a real-life penis, pulsing veins and all. It moved about my inner thighs, circling until it stopped, pausing over my clit and vibrating.

"Oh my gosh. This is the weirdest shit ever," I whispered, not bothering to stop it.

I arched my back as it rolled around my clit.

"Go inside," I said, testing to see if it was one of those magical objects that I could control, as I'd seen in Disney movies. But I wasn't telling a broom to sweep or a cake to bake. I was commanding this haunted, fake penis to bang me.

"Fuck me," I growled. "Now."

The toy slowly pulled away, edged itself down, and pushed itself inside of me, bobbing shallow thrusts.

"Deeper." I bucked my hips.

It followed my command, slamming into me until it all but disappeared inside of me.

"Shit. Don't stop. Do that." I reached down, rubbing my clit while it kept up a steady pace.

"This can't be happening," I whimpered, circling my clit faster. "I can't ... believe this." My breaths came out heavy.

Haunted Dildo fucked me so hard that my brain, along with the rest of my body, seemed to melt into a puddle of mush. I fought with my conscience, struggling to block out reality and enjoy this unreal moment so I could get my jollies.

I clenched down on the toy, working my fingers numb. I

needed to climax and wake up from this dream even if I couldn't remember falling asleep.

"Make me come," I whispered.

It grew thicker, pounded me harder, and even let out a grunt.

My legs twitched out to the sides, kicking over the pile of letters. I put my knuckles in my mouth and bit my lip hard. I couldn't help it. I was a very loud moaner, and the last thing I needed was Morningwood gossip about me flicking my bean.

My body bounced under the weight of something I couldn't see, like I was actually lying under a man who knew what he was doing. That magic dick stretched me out, pushing into me deeper and deeper until my eyeballs rolled into the back of my head and my entire body began to convulse. This was my fault for stuffing a magic fake dong into my own magic box. I'd made plenty of bad decisions before but none that resulted in me becoming possessed by a sex demon.

The blanket, the bed, and the room began to vibrate along with my body. I muffled my moans with my fist and let myself go. I thrashed against the toy, and it thrashed against me. Ripples of waves flushed from my toes to a tingle in my scalp as I came harder than I'd ever thought possible. I wasn't having just an orgasm. I was having a ground-breaking, full-body, pulsing, magical, weird, but fan-fucking-tastical experience. I was sure I'd wake up any moment now.

I panted, reaching down to pluck the toy from between my legs. It had already turned back into its plastic form. I brought it close to my face, inspecting it before laying it on the pillow and catching my breath. It twitched. I squinted my eyes and poked it.

"Too bad you don't do pillow talk after a banging like that," I muttered.

The room grew dark. Haunted Dildo began to roll around, jerking this way and that before letting out a loud pop and a sprinkle of confetti. A giant, shadowy figure emerged from the tip, bouncing around the room before landing in the chair across from me.

"Ta-da!" it said. "You liked that confetti, didn't you? I improvised that one."

I screamed, digging my heels into the bed and pushing myself to the headboard and as far away as possible from whatever the fuck I was looking at. If this were a dream, I still hadn't woken up. And if what had just happened couldn't wake me up, this all had to be real. I shook, chattering my teeth.

"Sorry. Sorry. No need to be scared! I sometimes forget to change to human form as soon as I'm released. Speaking of … how did I do? How was your release?" The shadow quickly transformed into a man—a very, very good-looking man. Dark hair, glowing eyes, devilish grin. Just the right amount of scruff along his jawline. He wore nothing but a pair of tight-fitting, steel-colored boxer briefs that clung to his ridiculously muscular body.

"What the hell are you? And what do you mean, my release?" I clutched the blankets under my chin as if I were nine again and hiding from monsters under my bed. Which, unless I had been slipped some kind of drug, that was precisely my situation. Except this monster looked a lot less scary and a lot more lickable.

My eyes drifted across his rippled abs and back up to his fiery gaze, which flickered, glowing in a way that wasn't humanly possible.

"Your release." He wiggled his brows. "You know what I'm talking about. I gave you a release, and you released me. Or … you rubbed one out. *Me*. You rubbed *me* out. I'm a genie.

Ta-da!" He threw his hands up and cocked his head to the side.

"This can't be happening. I'm dreaming. These small-town asshats are playing a trick on me. I think someone slipped a drug in the air or something." I closed my eyes, rubbing them hard before opening them again, expecting him to disappear.

"Still here." His voice fell flat.

"Fuck." I tried it again.

"Nope."

"Damn it. Why can't you go away?"

"You summoned me." He shrugged. "Look, you rubbed the magic dildo. You fucked me out. So, here I am. Your genie. All yours." He licked his lips, winking.

"Genies. Vampires. Werewolves. This shit isn't real." I shook my head, unable to take my gaze away from him. "I'm dreaming."

"Ugh," he groaned, rolling his eyes. "So, it's a vampire you want. Everyone wants a vampire these days. Ever since that damn Eduardo, Eddie, Ederdouche, whatever his name is. Vampires are as cold as a witch's titty. And believe me, I know how miserably cold that can be. Also, don't get me started on werewolves. All that hair! Ever had a pube in your mouth? Imagine licking a werewolf and getting one of their gnarly hairs stuck in your mouth. It's like sucking on a piece of dental floss without the minty-fresh feeling. Trust me. Unfortunately, I know how miserable that can be too. So, what I'm saying is, you got the best. Genies are awesome. At least, I am."

"Genie? You're a genie, living in a magic dildo?"

"Bingo! Now, you're getting it."

"I thought genies lived in lamps."

"Not this one. Hey, I'm not complaining. I know what

your heartbeat sounds like from the inside," he growled. "Tell me if a vamp or wolf can say that."

I bit my lip, still not convinced any of this was real.

"So, if you're a genie, do something magical."

"What more do you want? I just popped out of a dildo and transformed into this hot piece of ass before your eyes. Wow. You're a bit much to handle, lady. I don't even know your name. I'm Dylan, by the way. Kind of a big *dil* ... do. Ba-dum-cha." He played an invisible drum before slapping his knee and laughing at himself.

"I'm Claire. You can start your magic by giving me those three wishes that you're supposed to grant me, right?" I lowered the blanket, tucking it under my arms and covering myself.

"Oh." His shoulders slumped forward. "About that. Yeah, I can't. Or I could before, but I can't grant wishes anymore. I can try to make things work out in your favor, but it takes a lot of work on your end and mine. No wishes though, sorry. I'm kind of useless, I guess." He tapped his chin, staring up at the ceiling.

"What do you mean, you can't grant wishes? That's what genies do, I thought." I picked up the dildo, turning it in my palm to try and make sense of it.

"I'm a cursed genie. Cursed by an old flame. Karen." His voice trailed off.

"Karen Jackson?"

He gasped. "How did you know? Are you a witch?" His body began to fade in and out in a smoky blue haze.

"No. But Karen was my great aunt, and rumor has it that she was a witch."

"She was a witch all right—a coldhearted witch. Your great aunt is the reason you can't have your wishes. Sorry." He crossed his arms across his broad chest and huffed out a breath.

"Why? What did you do?"

"Why does it have to be something I did?"

"Well, you're the one she cursed."

"Fine, fine. I have this thing. For faeries. I was charmed, I swear!" He held his palms in the air. "Besides, it's not like we were in love. We weren't to that point yet. So, when that green fairy, Emry, came along with her soft emerald skin, things just happened. And by things, I mean, we clicked, meshed, and fucked. We had so much in common. I was trapped in a big blue dildo, and she was trapped in a bottle of absinthe. Once, your aunt was trying to rub me out, but I was over in Emry's bottle. I guess we were making a ruckus because she peered into that bottle, saw Emry facedown and ass up, and smashed the bottle against the wall."

I flinched. "Jeez. What happened to Emry? Didn't you get hurt?"

"No, I don't get hurt. I'm a genie! But Emry fled. No idea what happened to her. And after Karen cursed me to be useless and took away my wish power, I quit coming out for her. Anytime she rubbed me out, I'd run back inside my dildo. Witches be jealous."

"Ghosted. You ghosted her."

"I'm not a ghost." He flickered in and out like a bad signal on a television.

"No, it's a term for disappearing on someone. Relatively newish term. How long have you been in there anyway?" I nodded toward the dildo.

"Ah, let's see. The last thing I remember is the radio stations playing that damn 'Never Gonna Give You Up' song. Some guy named Rick. Hated that song. Always got stuck in my head." He hummed the tune, bobbing from side to side.

"The '80s." I sucked in my breath. "You have a lot to learn. So, tell me how the wish thing works. I can wish for anything?"

"Anything except the usual genie rules. No bringing back someone to life. I don't do zombies. Also, none of that love business. That's too messy. Oh, and you can't ask for more wishes. I think that covers it. But you're out of luck because I can't grant anything. Not unless we break this curse."

"And how do we do that?"

"We? Aha. So, you want those wishes, don't you?"

"Yes."

"I have to find my match." He shifted his fiery gaze out the window.

"Like, your twin? Your love match?"

"The matching piece to my blue dildo."

"Huh. That's weird. And then what?"

"No clue. I just know I used to have a match, and now, I don't. And your aunt said that was the only way I could return to my normal wish-granting state. I need that match with me."

"Okay. So, what am I searching for? Another dildo?"

"A matching blue butt plug," he stated.

"Are you serious?" I closed my eyes, pinching the bridge of my nose and sighing.

"I couldn't make this shit up."

# CHAPTER TWO

DYLAN

I FELL BACKWARD ONTO MY BED, THROWING MY ARMS OUT IN A sigh of relief. My dark, lonely dildo didn't seem as dark and lonely tonight. My entire room pulsed with the familiar glow that I'd once lost. Anytime someone summoned me, up until their wishes were granted, things were different. My surroundings vibrated, flashed, and twinkled with magic. But ever since Karen had taken my ability to grant wishes away, I was only a big, flashy dildo with mediocre tricks. I was useless.

*What kind of genie can't grant wishes?*

I'd been robbed of my geniehood all because I wanted a piece of that faerie ass. I should have known better. It was always the green faeries I needed to avoid. They were nothing but trouble.

"Claire," I whispered her name out like it was a single prayer. And it was.

She would save me from my pity party of one. At least, I hoped she would.

She sighed softly next to me, slightly jostling my room with each toss and turn. I knew I was the cause of her restless sleep. A sexy genie popping out of a dildo was beyond comprehension for most humans. But it was just another day in my magical realm.

We'd stayed up late as I tried to explain things to her, but skepticism had played across her face in the most seductive expression I'd known on any creature, human or not.

There was something about the way she'd focused that drove me wild. Her eyes would become hooded as she concentrated on what I told her. As if she needed to squint to hear my words correctly.

*"Let me get this right. You just came to be because you're just here? A big blue dildo. That's your story? Didn't someone make you? Do you remember life before being trapped in a dildo? Do you have parents? Do you have to stay inside there, or can you roam around? What're the rules?" She wrapped a sheet around her at the foot of the bed, propping herself up on her elbows and giving me her full attention.*

*I settled back into my chair and took a deep breath.*

*"No one has ever asked me all of these things before. Hmm. I'm pretty simple. I didn't have a life or anything before becoming a genie. I just was. Or am. I don't remember anything. No parents. We don't work like that. We aren't born into existence. We just are. Always were and always have been. As far as rules, I can't come out unless I'm summoned. Or rubbed. But then I can stay out until I fulfill my duties. Whatever that might be." I smirked, pointing finger guns at her and blowing a kiss.*

*She rolled onto her back, staring at the ceiling and groaning. "A genie that thinks he's a comedian. Just my luck. Too bad I can't write an article about this. They'd think I was batshit crazy. And maybe I am. Maybe, one day, I'll wake up from this weird dream."*

*"No deal, babe. It's real. I'm real. You're real. At least, what I felt of you was real." I stood up, stepping toward the bed—toward her. I stuck my hand out, running my palm up the length of her arm and hovering it over her collar before pulling back.*

*She sucked in her breath. "Yep. You're real."*


I slumbered hard after I returned to my dildo because that was what genies did. We slumbered. We didn't sleep, nap, or nod off. When my head hit the pillow, nothing could wake me, except a summons, unless I woke myself for one reason or another. And after my summoner first released me, she— or he—didn't need to rub me out anymore. I could appear or disappear at will until I granted their last wish. Then, I'd forever be just an ordinary dildo to them. I'd vanish from their life forever.

*Ghosted.*

I'd left that part out when I explained my genie rules to Claire. I didn't want her to know she could summon me without sticking me inside of her. It was a dick move, but then again, I was a dick. Literally.

My plan backfired as I paced my room for days before I felt the familiar pull again, sucking me out of my home and into the real world. I'd waited and waited on Claire to rescue me from my penis cage for what seemed like ages. After nothing but silence for days, I'd thought she'd given up. I couldn't blame her. She'd headed crotch-first into the magic world, and that was a scary thing.

She could run into all sorts of trouble, dabbling with the paranormal. She could frolic with demons, wrestle with ghosts, get hexed by a witch, and sit on a gnome. Once someone became aware of my world, they began to notice other things beyond human understanding too.

And sure enough, after a long drought of zero communication, she was rubbing one out, sending me flying back into her room—all razzly-dazzly and shit—and demanding answers.

"What's this? I walked across a bridge today, and look! Look!" She held the blanket over her naked body with one hand, and with the other, she shoved what looked like a phone in my face.

The screen had a snapshot of the ugliest, hairiest troll I'd ever seen. His brows were scrunched into his wrinkled hairline as he flipped off the camera.

"It's a troll. You can't just go walking over their bridges. Everyone knows that!" I crossed my arms, waiting on an explanation for her ghosting me.

"I've walked over that bridge dozens of times and never noticed that monster. I can't handle this. What do I need to do to go back to my world? I don't want to deal with any magic stuff anymore. I have a job to do."

"Yeah, you do if you want it all to stop. Find my magic butt plug."

"That's not the job I was talking about! I have an article to write. I need to save my career. Things aren't looking too good for me back home. I don't have time to go in search of a damn butt plug. I need to finish this article and go home, not set out on an adventure for a sex toy."

"Phew! You're on fire today. Are you sure that troll didn't cast a bad mood on you?"

She tightened the sheet around her. "Being here puts me in a bad mood. It's like the entire town has a curse on it. Everywhere I turn, people are gossiping or staring or just being overall annoying. I ran into two trolls today, by the way. The one under the bridge and one I went to high school with."

"You went to school with trolls? They're as dumb as rocks. I didn't know they went to school!"

"No, not a real troll. Just this girl. She used to bully me. She and her little group basically ran me out of this town. I never fit in anyway. I would sit under the trees, reading books, while all the other girls played soccer or braided their hair. I was a nerd. Still am a nerd. I just don't fit in here. It makes me uncomfortable to come back to this place. I need my info, and I need to go."

"Wish number one: become successful in your career. Wish number two: give that troll bitch a case of herpes. See? You know you want these wishes. Once we find that anal rammer, we'll be good to go." I flashed her a smile.

It usually wasn't difficult to talk someone into making wishes. But talking someone into finding a magic butt plug was proving harder than I'd imagined.

"Ugh!" She rolled out of bed, wobbling toward the bathroom and tripping over her sheet.

"Why are you covered up anyway? Think I haven't seen you before? Remember, I've seen you from the inside out. Kind of like you birthed me. That's weird. Erase that image from your mind. What I meant to say is, you're beautiful when you're mad. Come on and sit next to me." I patted the bed, beckoning her back to me. "We'll figure it out together. I need my geniehood back. I'm tired of being useless. You help me, and I'll help you. Can we make a deal? It shouldn't be hard to find the butt plug. Your aunt wasn't the brainiest witch around. I'm sure she stuffed it somewhere in her attic, basement, or shed. It seems to be stereotypical. Check those first."

"Look, you're nice."

*Uh-oh. Here we go. I've heard this tone before.*

"But I didn't fuck your big blue dick because I wanted you. I fucked it for answers."

"About that ... yeah, so ... you don't have to fuck yourself to summon me. Once you summoned me that first time, I'm good to go. Just stroke the dildo twice, and I'll appear. Sorry I forgot to mention that. But I'm here now, and you were just satisfied. Right? Are you not entertained?" I jumped up into the air, twirling in a smoky tornado swirl that I hoped would impress her.

She rolled her eyes. "You kept that from me on purpose!"

"Maybe."

"Back in you go," she snarled, stomping toward the bed and grabbing the plastic penis.

She stroked it twice, then twice more, and again and again.

"Why aren't you disappearing? Isn't that how I put you back in there too?"

"No. It's not even how you get me out. I just wanted to see if you'd really stroke it. That's pretty hot—and hilarious. Do it again. I felt that one in my cold, dead soul." I twitched, hovering a few feet off the bed.

"What a dick." She shook her head, tossing my home to the side.

"Duh." I smirked.

She lay down on the bed beside me, sighing. "What do I have to do to make you ghost me? Or if I need you to reappear? For research purposes, of course. So, I can get those wishes and get the hell out of Morningwood."

"I can come and go as I please. But if you want me gone forever, I need to grant those three wishes. After your last wish, I disappear. You couldn't even see me if you wanted to. Though I doubt you'd want to. Meow!" I clawed at the air.

Her eyes snapped to mine. "You mean, it all goes away? You go away and all the magic too?"

"Yep. The supernatural world will be closed off to you. Humans only get one genie per life. Even if you rubbed another magic dildo, nothing would happen. You could run into a vamp one day maybe or a shifter or something. But not likely. The rules of my world are different than yours. We're fully open or fully closed to those who seek us—or in your case, find us."

"I see. I'll head over to my mom's house in the morning. She lives in Great Aunt Karen's old place, where you came from. If you can appear and disappear, can you come with me? Help me out? It's your butt plug we're looking for anyway."

"Of course. Just stash me in your purse, and let's rock and roll."

"But you'll be quiet and not make an appearance unless she isn't around and all that, right? I can't have her seeing things. I don't need her holding anything else against me. She already guilt-trips me for being too good and leaving her behind."

"Is that true? Do you feel that way? That you're too good for the people here, even your mother?"

She picked the dildo up, stroking it back and forth in a fit of mock rage. "You're my genie, not my shrink. Now, get back into your penis, or I'll shove it in a troll's butthole."

I disappeared in a flash.

Literally.

I flash, banged, boomed the fuck outta there.

# CHAPTER THREE

CLAIRE

It had been years since I set foot in Great Aunt Karen's home. Even as a child, I'd feared visiting her. She babysat me on days when my mom worked weekends. Those weekends were the most dreaded times of my childhood. Great Aunt Karen would set me to cleaning her home, inside and out, the entire time. Only about thirty minutes before my mother picked me up would she lay out over-steeped tea and stale butter cookies, as if we had been lounging, reading books, and savoring snacks all day.

Not that my mother would care. I'd been the only one to clean our house too. The moment Annie left work, she'd come home and pour herself a whiskey. She'd sit at the kitchen table and drone on and on about her day while I boiled whatever canned food we could afford. On Mondays and Wednesdays, I'd heat canned ravioli. The *plop* sound it made as it slid a slimy trail out of the can and into our only frying pan would forever haunt my memories. I'd not eaten ravioli since I left Morningwood.

I'd hover over the stove, pretending to listen to my mom's woeful tales, but my mind would drift elsewhere. In a book. In a dream. Somewhere far away. After dinner, I'd wash the dishes and put them away. By the time I finished tidying up, she would be lying down, passed out on the couch already. More often than not, a burning cigarette in her hand. I'd stub it out, tiptoeing past her and into my room to read. I couldn't escape my world fast enough.

I'd lose myself in tales of fantastical things, such as creatures from the sea, majestic unicorns, princely knights, and non-slutty green faeries. I loved living in a fantasyland, even if it existed only in my imagination. But now that a real-life fantasy had fallen into my hands, I refused to accept it. I'd given up on fairy tales long ago. Now, things such as trolls, witches, and Dylan were more of a hassle than the dreamy realm I'd escaped to long ago.

"Think we can swing by somewhere to eat? I've not had food in decades!" Dylan asked, drumming his fingertips across his knee. He'd promised that he would behave if I let him hang out instead of hiding.

"Genies eat?" I pulled out of the hotel parking lot in my rental car.

The only rental company in Morningwood was Fat Sal's. Fat Sal had been around for years, providing cars to the four tourists we had each season. But lately, as word had gotten out that our town topped the charts as one of the most haunted places in America, Fat Sal's business had slowly been growing. She'd happily informed me she had a total of eight cars now instead of five.

I liked Fat Sal. She didn't treat me like the rest of the townsfolk. She probed and prodded me out of curiosity, not to use my words as ammunition for small-town gossip. I knew because she was also an outcast. She'd left town twenty years ago but had to come back to take care of her ailing mother. The townsfolk never forgave her for leaving. I had no idea how her business had stayed afloat for so long, but when she'd told me things were good, I couldn't help but feel a sense of victory. At least one of us was sticking it to the shitty people here.

"No, we don't eat. But we can. Do they still make those Mack Daddy things?" he asked, rubbing his palms together. His biceps flexed with each movement beneath his tight-fitting tee.

Before we'd left the hotel, I'd had to explain to him that wind suits were now out of fashion. When he'd emerged from the dildo, wearing something that looked like a tattered purple parachute, I couldn't help but laugh. He'd magically poofed through several outfits before I settled on a basic tee and jean combo—my favorite look on a man. Not that I was checking him out. Not really. He was a genie, and I was a human. I didn't know much about the fantastical world, but I knew enough to know that I couldn't have a relationship with a genie. Besides, he had a thing for naughty faeries, not nerdy journalists.

"Mack Daddy? What's that?"

"You know, the meat and the bun. Pickles, lettuce, tomato. Something-something sesame seeds." His voice trailed off into song.

"Big Mac. You're thinking about a Big Mac. It's a burger," I groaned, taking a sharp left toward our only McDonald's.

"Yeah, that! With fries and a milkshake. I dip my fries into my milkshake. Do you do that? I learned that trick from your great aunt. Thought maybe it ran in the family. Hope that jealous-fit-of-rage streak doesn't though." His body flashed blue before returning back to a normal human color.

"Why? Plan on fucking any faeries?"

"Look, I'm just saying, we don't know what we'll find in that attic. Or the basement. Or wherever we look. We might find a succubus," he growled. "Always wanted to take one of them to Pound Town."

My fingers curled tight around the steering wheel.

"Humans don't do it for you?" I asked.

"Didn't say that. I can get off to anything, even centaurs. Don't ask. That was a weird kink phase of my life." He rolled down the window, sticking his head out the side like a dog. "Damn, this fresh air feels so good!"

"Get back in here! What if someone sees you!" I tugged his arm, pulling him back into the car.

"Relax. I'll be on my best behavior. No one knows I'm a genie. I look like an ordinary man, right?" He ran his hand through his hair, shaking it out in slow motion.

"Yep. Normal," I lied, pressing my lips together.

There was nothing ordinary about the way Dylan looked. Not the way he carried himself, his posture, or his deep voice that vibrated on every syllable. This creature wasn't like any man I'd known.

"Your eyes give you away. They flicker. Like a flame." I shrugged my shoulders.

"They are flames. Check it out." He leaned into me.

I caught a whiff of his intoxicating, woodsy, smoky, manly, extremely real-life-human scent, and my car ran off the road.

"I'm trying to drive!" I cried, veering back into my lane.

"Sorry! Sorry! I forgot. Humans can die. Shit! Well, along those lines, we can too. When these flames go out, I go out." He leaned back in his seat.

"What? I thought you were immortal?"

"Kind of. I reincarnate. It's never happened, obviously. I'm still a genie living in a dildo and not a human in a Manhattan apartment, living a posh life. But hey, I like this genie thing. For the most part. When I'm summoned anyway.

Otherwise, staying cooped up in a room by myself for decades can be a drag."

"How do you know you can reincarnate if it's not happened?" I pulled into the drive-through line.

"Damn, you're full of questions for someone who wants this magic business out of her life." He raised his brows before dipping his head to read the menu.

"I'm just curious, is all. Is there some special genie network, and you guys know all the things?"

"First of all, it's guys and gals. There are women genies. And second of all, yes. That's exactly what it is. We share information. We come into the world with it—it somehow appears in our brain—and we just know things. Like, for instance, I know that eating human food will make me feel like shit. But it's so good that I'm going to do it anyway. I learned that through the telepathic genie line eons ago, but it's never stopped me from trying. Like now. I'll take the Mack Daddy meal with a chocolate milkshake, please. Never vanilla. I'd give you cash, but I haven't worked in the history of ever. Sorry! Oh, and a tea to go, too, please."

The thought of tea brought my mind back to Great Aunt Karen's place. I swallowed hard, losing my appetite. I pulled up to the intercom and ordered our meals, paid for them, and sped off toward my mom's place while Dylan simultaneously hummed and munched next to me. He dipped his fries in his milkshake and inhaled them as if he'd been starving for the last decade.

He tore the lid off of his tea and gulped down the drink, licking his lips before speaking again, "You know, another one of my abilities is that I'm able to pick up on things." He pulled his burger out and ate it in a handful of bites.

"Like an empath?" I asked.

I veered left down a gravel drive, glancing into the rearview mirror at the smoky trail of dust I'd left behind.

The familiar sound of rocks under my tires caused the hair at the nape of my neck to stand on end.

"No clue what that is. Dumb it down for me." He wiped his hands on a napkin before rolling the empty foil wrapper into a ball and stuffing it back into the bag.

"You can feel other people's emotions, and it affects you. Basically."

"Hmm. I guess so. It doesn't affect me that much though. Or it hasn't. But I'm feeling you out right now. You're anxious. Scared. Terrified even."

"And that makes you anxious, scared, and terrified?" I pulled in front of the dilapidated clapboard house. It looked the same as it had when I was younger, like a pillar of dread. White paint chipped off the wood in flecks as big as my hands, exposing a grayish-bone-hued tone, as if the home had shed its skin to expose its skeleton. I shivered, turning the engine off.

"No. It makes me feel protective. Angry even. Vengeful." His eyes flickered in a blaze of lightning, blinding me like a doe-eyed dumbass in headlights. His growl came out thick, like a low rumble of thunder.

He reached for my hand, pulling me back into my seat. I hadn't realized I was trying to open the door and run.

"Something's here. I don't like it. Why do you feel anxious? Did something happen to you here?"

"No. Nothing too terrible. I just always had a sense of dread, coming here. Great Aunt Karen used to treat me like Cinderella. *Do this and do that*, she'd say. I worked my knuckles raw, scrubbing her floors and her tubs. She was never grateful. She only sneered at me, laughing and calling me stupid. Telling me I'd never amount to shit. She'd say I was as dumb as the sponge I used to clean her bath. I never had the backbone to stand up to her. I don't know how you two were ever a thing. How could you like someone like that? That lady was—"

"A jealous witch. I recall her telling me about a girl helping around here from time to time. That must have been you. It was on those days that she'd lock me up inside the box. She didn't want me to see you. I don't need my magical abilities to see that Karen was jealous of you. Even when you were younger, she knew how beautiful you were. And intelligent and that you were going places and she'd stay here in this rotten place for good.

"As far as my relationship with her, Karen had charmed me. She was a good witch until she was a bad witch. I had no idea of her split-personality complex until she found me banging Twinkerballs. Dodged a bullet with that one, I'd say. We both did. You left, and I hid."

"Thanks. That's really nice of you to say." I took a deep breath, gathering whatever little courage I had before heading inside.

I'd called my mother earlier and let her know I was coming, but she said she wouldn't be back for a while. She'd left a key under the doormat, warning me that her place was a mess and not to judge her.

*Too late, Ma.*

Her absence alone should have calmed me. But the sense of dread still gnawed at me, bubbling into my throat like invisible hands slowly strangling me from the inside out.

"You'll be fine. Nothing's going to hurt you when I'm around. Besides, that old witch is gone. How'd she die anyway? Burning at the stake, I hope." Dylan's assurance smoothed over me like a blanket of calm—my own personal anxiety blanket.

"Old age, I guess. A friend found her in bed. I think she died in her sleep. The friend phoned my mom to let her know, and that was that. She was buried and this house was passed down to my mom, Annie. Not sure if Karen ever mentioned her."

"No. Never heard the name. I didn't even know Karen had friends. She seemed like a loner to me—content in her own little world out here, in the middle of nowhere. Gosh, I hate seeing this place again, probably as much as you do. I knew something was up when I felt myself jostling around in that box. I'd been lying in the damn attic for too long to be back so quickly." He stretched his back before slumping his shoulders and sighing. "Let's get this over with. Let's find that magic butt plug and get you those wishes. You'll be out of this forsaken town before you know it. Just drop me off somewhere beforehand, please. Maybe Tahiti or Paris. I heard French girls ... ya know." He wiggled his brows.

"Ugh. *Oui, oui.* Let's go." I rolled my eyes and opened the door, forcing myself out of the car.

# CHAPTER FOUR

DYLAN

WHATEVER UNEASINESS FELL UPON CLAIRE FELL UPON ME TOO. I'd picked up on her vibes as soon as we turned down the long, gravel drive. Her fear had me on high alert. There was no telling what could be lurking in the depths of Karen's house. Maybe she'd cursed the place with a spell that even my sick mind couldn't imagine. My nostrils flared as we stepped inside the house. I'd made Claire walk behind me as I led her up the stairs.

The air hung heavy with the smell of ashtrays and something rotting. I unfolded the wooden ladder and gently nudged Claire upstairs before I floated to the top.

"No fair. Must be nice to float around lazily," Claire said.

"It does have its perks. I can still do a few tricks." I swung my hand in the air, releasing a string of butterflies.

"Useful." She pressed her lips into a thin line and nodded. "What does it look like?" she asked, pulling a cardboard box over toward the window, plopping herself down beside it, and rummaging.

"Like a big blue butt plug. Don't you know what that looks like?" I paused, peering over a stack of boxes.

Sunlight filtered through the window, illuminating her golden locks in a bright, glowing halo.

"I guess I thought maybe it would be in a trashy jeweled box like you were in."

"Did you just call my dildo trash? How dare you. Rude!" I opened a box of old curtains and pillowcases, setting it aside.

"No. I didn't say dildo. I said box. I assumed that since your magic toy lived in a box, she might have put the other magic toy in a fancy box too. Makes sense." She shrugged, closing the box. "It's not in this one. Hand me another." She shoved it to the side.

"I don't know if she put it in there or not. Knowing her, she probably buried herself with it." I kicked another box toward her.

"I'm not digging up my great aunt to pull a butt plug from her ass. So, don't even ask," she muttered.

"Ew! Who said she had it in her ass? Gosh, Claire. Where's your mind? I thought she'd clutched it in her fist, and we would have to pry it from her cold, dead hand. Not dig it from her skeleton butt," I said.

She giggled, reaching inside another box. I felt her change in mood as a warm tingle spread throughout my body.

"Was that a giggle? I don't think I've heard that before. Do it again. It felt good." I stepped closer to her, perching on an old wooden chair prickled with splinters.

She threw her head back, opened her mouth wide, and let out a high-pitched guffaw before turning back to me with a satisfied grin. "Ask and you shall receive."

"So, you do have a funny bone in there. I thought you were Little Miss Serious. But I think I'm wrong. You can be as silly as me. Muahahaha." I let out a deep, rumbling, throaty, evil laugh.

"Just because my dark sense of humor shows herself every once in a while doesn't mean I can be as silly as you. You're on a *twelve-year-old boy* level. I'm closer to fifteen." She winked, tossing another box aside.

"I can't tell if you're flirting with me or insulting me, but I'll take it. You're making my body feel all warm and fuzzy." I leaped in the air, twirling in my most majestic genie moves.

"Definitely insulting." She pointed to the last stack of boxes in the corner and snapped her fingers.

"I'm your genie, not your slave. Sheesh. I poked my head in those already. Nothing's in there but old photos. Let's try the basement. Chop-chop." I snapped my fingers back at her.

"I'll meet you down there. Let me take a quick look around some closets and drawers." She pushed herself off the floor, arching her back in one long stretch.

"I'll wait."

"No. Why? It'll go faster if we're in two places at once. Plus, my mom is a mess. You don't need to help me with her junk."

"I don't care about your mom's hygiene or cleaning habits. I feel that dread again. I'm not leaving you alone." I stepped aside, letting her climb down the attic ladder.

"I'll be fine. I just get the heebie-jeebies from that basement, is all. That's what you're feeling."

I floated down toward her, blocking her path. "No. I don't think you need to be alone in this house. I'm getting an unsettling feeling, and it's not just coming from you. I'm your genie. I'm a part of you until I'm not. You're safest with me." I reached out, cupping her shoulders with my palms and forcing her to look into my eyes.

"Okay." She lowered her lashes, staring at her worn-out tennis shoes. "Let's get the basement over with first then. I want to get out of here soon. If she hid it somewhere, she wouldn't want it found. I'm sure it's in that damn creepy basement." She turned on her heels, walking back downstairs and toward the basement door.

Empty bottles of liquor lay strewn about the kitchen countertop with half-eaten molded toast, shriveled strawberry tops, and a coffee pot full of filmed-over coffee.

She blushed, waving away the mess. "My mom is ... going through some things. As usual. Sorry it's disgusting in here."

"You don't have to apologize to me. Not like I have to live here anymore. I also know you won't send me back to this grave. Not after I dazzle you with your wishes. You'll be forever grateful." I put my hand on her lower back, steering her around the mess.

"You sure are confident in yourself. But you're right. I'll send you somewhere nice. Maybe the next woman who rubs one out will be the one for you. The forever one. She'll have big, bouncy boobs, a round and perky ass, and fuck you like your green faerie girl." Her voice trailed off as she opened the creaky basement door and flicked on the light.

"Stop. Let me go first." I put my arm out and pushed her back behind me. "Something's in there. I can feel it."

"What do you mean, something's in there?"

"That dread you're feeling. It's coming from the basement. It could be a wight, a ghost, a demon. I don't know, but I'm about to get rid of it for good."

"You can do that? What if you get hurt? You can't leave me alone here!" She tugged my shoulder, pulling me backward. "Please," she whispered.

"I'll be back," I said in my best robotic impression of that weird movie Karen had made me watch long ago.

"Damn it, Dylan. This isn't a time to be silly! I'm scared." She wrung her hands, shifting her weight from one foot to the other.

"And nothing down here scares my lady like that," I growled before ripping my shirt off and throwing it behind me. I closed my eyes, concentrating on making myself twice as big as my usual size. I stooped, narrowly avoiding my head crashing into the ceiling.

"I had no idea you could do that," she said, craning her neck to look up at me.

"I wasn't sure I still could. It's been a while. Stay put. I'll check it out." I disappeared down the stairs, eyes ablaze.

I dodged the dim, useless lightbulb that hung from the rafters and made my way toward the back. I hovered inches above the ground, not wanting to risk stepping on something that could reach out and grab my leg before I had a chance to attack first. I'd fought evil creatures before, and I'd do it again. But I was taking precautions with Claire. If something happened to her on my watch, I'd never forgive myself. I wanted to end her adventures in the magical world as much as she did. Life in this realm was too dangerous for her. But then again, I'd never see her again after that third wish. She'd disappear from me as soon as I said *abracadabra*.

I suppressed a sigh, slowly inching forward. The scent of mildew mixed with something rotten grew heavy, lingering in the air and stifling my breaths.

*Scratch. Scratch. Scratch.*

Something scratched from the back corner. I paused, listening again.

*Scratch. Scratch. Scratch.*

My eyes grew brighter, slowly lighting the path before me. Whatever beast was making that noise was much too big to be a mouse and, thankfully, much too small to be a skeleton.

*Scratch. Scratch. Scratch.*

I puffed out my chest and took a few steps forward.

*Scratch.*

I floated above a small skull, a mound of fur, and tiny bones littering the cement floor. When I'd lived with Karen, she'd always complained about the rats in her basement. But now, I was beginning to think she'd had a bigger problem than rodents.

*Scratch. Scratch.*

"A wiggity wiggity wack," a low, nasally voice called out.

"Did someone just say, *wiggity wiggity wack?*" I asked, hesitating before I took another step forward.

"Welcome to my crib, bruh. That's me. Big Glug-Glug," the voice answered.

*Scratch. Scratch.*

I cast my eyes to the far corner, illuminating the fattest goblin I'd ever seen. His bulbous nose bent down in the shape of a flaccid penis. He bobbed his round body side to side while scratching records on a turntable nestled between his beefy thighs.

*Scratch. Scratch. Scratch.*

"Right. Big Glug-Glug. Uh, what are you doing here?" I scratched my head.

I'd had my fair share of dealings with goblins, but those encounters had been frightening. Big Glug-Glug looked like he'd require a forklift to pry him from the ground.

"I could ask the same of you. Why you down here, disturbing my recording studio? I'm trying to make a rap song. Scratching records and shit, bruh. I had it going good until you came along, distracting me with your big-ass, floaty smoke bag." The goblin reached behind himself, picked up what looked like a squirrel's tail, and took a bite.

"Floaty smoke bag? I don't look like a bag!" I crossed my arms over my chest. "I didn't mean to disturb your, uh, rap session. I'm searching for something. I'll be out of your way in just a moment."

"Dylan? Are you speaking to someone? I'm coming down. I found a flashlight," Claire said. Her footsteps echoed down the stairs. The bright light in her hand bounced back and forth off the walls as she ran toward me.

"Come on over. You're safe," I called back.

"Man, what? How do you know y'all are safe? I'm hard. I'm a goblin. I can fuck yo shit up. See that pile of bones right there? That was a rat family. Used to be my good friends. But then I ate 'em." Big Glug-Glug pointed at a few scattered bones beside him.

"Why would you do that?" I looked back behind me, motioning for Claire.

"They ratted me out," he answered.

*Scratch. Scratch. Scratch.*

Claire screamed, dropping the flashlight. It rolled toward Big Glug-Glug, who took one look at it and ate it in a single gulp.

"What the hell did you do that for?" I threw my hands in the air.

"My soul's too dark. I needed to brighten it up in there a little. These lyrics ain't coming as fast these days. I need inspo. That hot little piece of ass you got there might help me out though." He nodded his swollen face toward Claire, who stepped behind me.

"Claire, meet Big Glug-Glug, the goblin rapper. Big Glug-Glug, meet Claire, my summoner."

"This is fucking ludicrous!" she gasped, still hiding behind me.

"Hell no, woman. I'm not Ludacris. I'm Big Glug-Glug. My rhymes are straight fresh." He groaned, lifting his leg and letting out one long-drawn-out fart. "Rat bastards do that to me."

Claire recoiled, gagging. Even I felt my Mack Daddy burger rising in my throat.

I leaned down, whispering in her ear, "Goblins are even

more disgusting than trolls, just FYI. But this one might be able to help us."

"Good. Let's get the info and get out of here before I get sick," she whispered back.

"Yo, yo, yo! No secrets around here. Snitches get stitches." He shook his head, shaking loose a fly out of his unibrow.

*Scratch. Scratch.*

"No secrets. We're discussing what we came here for. We're looking for a butt plug." I pressed my lips into a thin line. There was simply no way to ask politely about a butt plug, and given that I was speaking with a dirty goblin, I didn't much care about manners anyway.

"Old lady Karen's nasty blue butt plug, eh? I wrote a rap about that thing once." He grinned, showing us a mouthful of rotted teeth.

"I don't even want to know. Can you just tell us where it might be?" Claire stepped forward.

"For a price, honey. Always for a price," he hissed, licking his lips with a slimy, forked tongue.

"Name it. I need that butt plug," she said.

"I want Bruno's gold chain. Bring it to me, and I'll tell you where your filthy treasure lies."

*Scratch.*

"Shit. I hope you're up for an adventure," I muttered to her.

"Why? Who is Bruno?" Her eyebrows pulled together.

"The bogeyman. The swamp boss. He's not going to give that chain up easily. It's magic." I rubbed my palms over my face.

"I wouldn't expect it to be anything else. Of course it's magic. Goblins, bogeymen, genies, faeries." She blew out a loud breath through her flared nostrils.

Her frustration bounced off of me.

I reached down, patting the top of her head before

squinting my eyes and shrinking to my average size. "There. That's better. Now, I can be on your level and see that pretty face of yours." I tipped her chin up, smiling to try and lighten the mood, but tears began to brim in her eyes. I put my arms around her and pulled her close. "Hey. I'll end this for you soon. I'm sorry I turned your life upside down. I'll get you back to work and richer or more powerful or whatever your command is. I promise. Genies can't break promises. Now, let's get you out of here and take you home."

# CHAPTER FIVE

## CLAIRE

I HADN'T WANTED TO GO BACK TO THE HOTEL AFTER LEAVING my mom's place, but Dylan had insisted on it. When I'd seen that flame burn brighter in his eyes and the firm set of his jaw, I hadn't had the energy to argue. Besides, I didn't know the extent of his power. He couldn't grant wishes, but I'd seen him appear and reappear in a cloud of smoke and grow three times his size in a flash. He could probably do anything he wanted with me. I didn't want to piss off anyone who could transform me into a toad, a washed-up old hag, or a ball gag to match his set of sex toys.

I paced the room and tried to gather myself before we set out again. The swamp wasn't a far drive from Creaky Spring Inn, according to Dylan. I paused in front of the closet door's mirror, scaring myself. I'd been so distracted with this new normal that I'd completely forgotten to brush my hair, wash my face, and tweeze my brows. I looked like I'd just crawled out of a grave.

"Jeez Louise! Why didn't you tell me I looked like a hot

mess?" I put my head in my hands, hiding my face that desperately needed a swipe of lipstick, a curl of lashes, or a face transplant with someone way less tired.

"What? Louise? I'm Dylan. And besides, you look fabulous. But ..." He sat on the edge of the bed, brushing crumbs off the sheets.

"But what?"

"But you aren't dressed for the swamp. Or The Cave rather." He clasped his chin between his fingers before snapping. "Aha!"

"What do you mean, I'm not dressed for a swamp or cave? Do I need wading boots and camouflage?" I put my hands on my hips. I wanted to get out of here and get this show on the road. I needed that butt plug.

"Hardly. Close your eyes. This might get bright."

He held out his hands and wiggled his fingers, sending a flash of bright light through the room, blinding me. My body spun around more times than I could count.

I gasped, digging the base of my palms into my eye sockets. "I can't see! And I'm dizzy! What the hell?"

"You can open your eyes now." He pulled my hands from my face.

I stood still, my vision slowly adjusting through the cloud of smoke swirling around me. A chill raked across the back of my thighs, sending shivers up my spine.

"Eh?" He nodded his head up and down in an exaggerated movement while pointing at my outfit. "Now, you fit in."

I looked down at the black vinyl boots, the black vinyl corset, and the black vinyl booty shorts clinging to my bare skin. Fingerless spiked-leather gloves reached up to my elbows, and a heavy gunmetal chain hung around my neck. I clasped a long, roped whip in my palm.

"What the fuck is this shit, Dylan? Fix it. Turn me back." I cracked the whip above his head.

He recoiled, grabbing his sides in a fit of laughter.

As a child, I'd imagined myself in that Cinderella moment when the fairy godmother conjured a beautiful ballgown for her—a ballgown, not a dominatrix outfit.

"You look sinful," he growled, pulling me into him. "Just one last thing." He flicked the top of my head, sprouting two curled black horns from my scalp.

I blinked, turning back toward the mirror. I pricked my finger on the sharp tips of my horns to check if they were real.

"This isn't funny anymore," I cried.

"Actually, it is. But it's not just fun and games. You have to fit in or else we're toast." He licked his lips, focusing on my breasts that spilled over the tight corset. "Tonight, I'm just a genie bringing my sexy succubus to The Cave. You wouldn't gain entrance as a human, and it would arouse suspicion. Besides, you look edible."

"Am I a part of some type of sex trade or something? What's The Cave? I thought we were only stealing a chain from the bogeyman?" My heart began to race.

"There you go, getting anxious again. I can feel it." He straightened his back, grabbing my hand. "I told you, I'll keep you safe. This is part of that. Just trust me on this. It's hard to explain until you see it with your own eyes. You wouldn't believe me." He shook his head, turning toward the door. "I'll go down and distract the workers while you sneak in the car with your dominatrix outfit. I know how you're afraid of what these small-minded townsfolk will say. Wait for me out front. Give me five minutes. When you hear my signal, run and start the engine."

"What's the signal?" I spit out, crossing my arms over my chest. I accidentally popped a boob out, causing Dylan to moan before I could quickly stuff it back into my tiny top. "Get it together. It's just a boob."

"Right. Just a boob." He adjusted his pants. "Um, not sure yet on the signal. But you'll know it when you hear it." He disappeared in a cloud of blue vapor before I could ask him anything else.

I glanced at my reflection in the mirror again, admiring the shiny vinyl. I never wore much of anything besides jeans and T-shirts or the occasional summer dress. But this outfit looked hot, and that feisty side of me that had long since disappeared began to awaken again. I ran my palms down the slick material, turning this way and that. My jaw dropped as I noticed a tail swishing out from behind me, posing in the air like a snake on the verge of striking. I grinned, distracted by my new toy when I heard the signal.

Someone was loudly beatboxing into a megaphone.

I groaned, grabbing my purse, my keys, and my tail before making a run for the car. I flew past the empty lobby and out the door. Dylan popped up behind me, quickly following on my heels. We reached the car, hopping inside before anyone spotted us. I turned the key in the ignition and floored the gas pedal, peeling out of the parking lot. We made it down the street before we both caught our breath.

"Like my rap? Think I can sell it to Big Glug-Glug?" Dylan asked between heavy breaths.

"I thought you were going to whistle or meow. You know, like a normal person," I answered.

"But I'm not a person. I'm a genie. Ta-da!" He snapped his fingers.

My chest flew into the steering wheel as two enormous claw-tipped wings emerged from my back, stretching out into the front seat and smacking Dylan under his nose.

"Oh. Didn't think this through," he said, clutching the dashboard as I swerved into a ditch.

"You could have gotten us killed! I can't drive like this!" I grabbed my wing, desperately trying to stuff it down behind me.

I'd always wondered what it would feel like to have wings. I'd sometimes imagined myself with beautiful butterfly wings or angelic fluffy, feathered ones—not demon wings complete with demon horns.

"That's fine. We're here anyway. Told ya it was close. Just straighten the car out, and let's go. You have to relax, and your wings will settle."

I snarled, reversing the car and parking it alongside the ditch in short, jerking movements to emphasize how pissed off I was becoming. I was never much one for vocal confrontation.

"I had to give you wings, Claire. You're a succubus. They have wings, and we can't blow your cover. You can't look like a human. You already smell like one."

"What's that supposed to mean? What do I smell like?" I pushed the door open, struggling to get myself out of the car.

"To me, you smell like raw, human emotion. Sweet breaths of life. And pure, carnal sex. You're the most delicious-scented human I've ever smelled. But to them, you'll probably smell like a mortal. Like death lingers on your shoulders." He walked over to me, grabbing my wings and pushing them down. "Relax."

I flapped them in response, sending my feet flying a few inches off the ground before I crashed back down into the mud.

"You're as stubborn as your great aunt. That's for damn sure. Follow me and put those things down. I don't have time to teach you how to fly. I'm not sure how long my magic will hold. I've only magicked another human twice before, and it didn't last long."

He grabbed my arm, pulling me through a thicket and into an overgrown meadow. The long blades of grass swayed in the wind, hitting me under my chin and tickling my collar. The sky grew darker with each step I took until I could no longer see much of anything in front of me.

"I'm not stubborn! Not really. I just can't believe I'm on a quest to find a magic butt plug," I huffed, clutching my hand around Dylan's bicep and slowly following behind him. "I used to love fairy tales. I read about them all the time as a child. I wanted to live in those worlds. Now, I realize how dumb that was. I mean, look at us. We're out here, in the middle of nowhere, heading toward a cave I didn't even know existed. And why is it dark all of a sudden? It was daylight when we got out of the car. I can't see a damn thing now. Oh. Spooky, spooky." I fluttered my fingers in the air, mocking my ridiculous situation.

"Shh! You don't know what's lurking out here," Dylan said.

He moved his palm back and forth, magically bending the grass apart and creating a path for us to walk through. We stopped at the edge of a swamp. My boots began to sink quickly in the sticky mud. Dylan's eyes blazed bright enough for me to notice a path of jagged rocks sticking out of the water.

"Stereotypical. We have to hop the stones to get to a magic cave where this bogey-douche lives. You know, I always thought this town was lame, but this takes the cake. At least throw a dragon in there or something."

"Hell no! We're not fighting dragons. Besides, I don't think a stone path is stereotypical. Neither is Bruno." Dylan motioned for me to follow him, hopping from one stone to the next.

"What? He isn't a hairy monster who lives under my bed?" I rolled my eyes.

"Does this look like under your bed?"

"Well, no, but—"

"I know your first taste of the magical realm was me. And I admit, I'm a catch. *I can show you my magical world,*" he sang before clearing his throat. "Sorry. Old habits. Anyway, like I was saying, I'm fun, I'm playful, I'm sexy. But I'm not harmless. And neither is anyone else, friend or foe, that you'll come across. Big Glug-Glug back there can eat you in two bites. He looked small and gross, but goblins can unhinge their jaws like a snake. And their stomach acid can burn their victims up in seconds. It's pretty disgusting. I watched one swallow a centaur once. That was a nightmare I try to forget."

"What's so scary about you? You said you're not harmless. I doubt you'd hurt a fly."

I lost my footing, slipping on a rock. He turned in a flash, caught me in one arm, and pulled me into him. I gasped, clinging to his shoulders and heaving against his chest.

"Careful there, princess. Just one slip into that murky water, and you'll be sick for weeks. As I said, don't let anything fool you. Nothing is harmless, especially Morningwood." The fire in his gaze grew brighter, causing me to shield my eyes before he turned away.

I hesitated, wanting to know more about his powers and what caused him to be so scary, according to him. But a faint bassline thumped through the swamp, and neon lights flashed in the distance, distracting me from caring.

"What's that? A party?"

My wings fluttered behind me, causing me to slip again. He reached out, steadying me.

"That's The Cave." A devilish grin played across his face.

"That's The Cave? Like Bogey-dude's place? What is it, a nightclub?" My eyes grew wide. I'd prepared myself to navigate a dark, disgusting, damp, moldy cave—not a disco rave.

"That's exactly what it is. Bruno owns it. He is literally a *boogie-*man. As in *get down on it.* The Cave is the most popular club in the South—or it used to be the last time I left my dear ol' dildo. You'll see. Be prepared to see some wild shit. But"— his eyes flared—"stay close to me. Don't you dare leave my side. Remember, this place and these people aren't harmless. Let me do the talking with Bruno."

I nodded silently. I couldn't speak if I wanted to. Things kept growing weirder and weirder, and I couldn't tell if I felt more nervous or excited. A magical nightclub sounded like fun. But it also seemed like trouble. I wasn't good at either of those things.

"Oh, and one last thing. Sorry for this, but—" He puffed a cloud of stale smoke in my face.

I gagged, grabbing my sides and heaving before the vapor disappeared.

"What was that for?" Tears streamed down my face. I tried to pat them dry with my vinyl gloves, but it was useless. I only slicked the wetness down my cheeks.

"You smell too lovely, babe. Better safe than sorry. The scent will wear off with my magic. Come on. Let's go before that happens." He grabbed my hand, pulling me toward the music.

I hopped from rock to rock, following him until we stood before a giant cave. At the top hung a neon-green sign that read, *The Cave.*

*Original,* I thought.

Peering over his shoulder and leaning toward the mixture of sounds coming from inside, I heard laughter, moans, screams, and a shrill noise that jarred my jaw, causing me to clench my teeth.

"Banshee. Tune it out. You ready?" He gazed down at me. His eyes blazed, burning my face like I'd opened a furnace ... or looked toward the sun.

"I think so." I gulped.

"You asked me what I could do that was harmful."

He grabbed my shoulders and spun me around to face the path we'd just crossed. The entire swamp lit up in a quick flash of fre, painfully heating the vinyl against my skin. The blue flames disappeared before I could blink.

"You're safe with me," he growled.

I bit my lip, realizing another stereotypical cliché in my new fairy-tale life. I was beginning to see Dylan in a whole new ligh.

# CHAPTER SIX

DYLAN

My last encounter with Bruno had ended in disaster, thanks to Karen.

She'd heard about the infamous bogeyman and wanted to see his skills for herself.

*She drove us to The Cave on a sudden whim. We arrived and meandered our way through crowds, heading toward the back of the club, where he sat, surrounded by a pack of werewolves. We sat across from his table, downing fire cider and spooky juice while trying to figure him out. Karen studied his actions while I studied the dancing faeries flying through the air in front of me.*

*I couldn't help it. They seductively swung their hips back and forth, distracting me from the odd performance onstage. The crowds had gathered around a creature I'd not seen before. He was as tall as a giant but as dark as a demon. He had human features, but something ethereal lurked underneath his skin. He emerged* from behind a curtain, wearing nothing but a robe. His feet seemed to glide across the floor as he danced in tune with the music. He paused, as if waiting for a cue. A long-legged elf, also dressed in only a robe, joined him onstage. She was a night elf with moonlit eyes and skin the color of twilight. Her ears stuck out from behind silver-hued locks.

The music raged on, and the lights kept flashing as the two creatures twirled around each other. I sat in a trance, my mission with Karen long since forgotten. As far as I was concerned, I was here to party, not study some old, washed-up monster.

The elf dropped her robe, exposing her petite breasts. Her nipples were dark as midnight. The crowd chanted from below, grinding up against each other.

The giant creature licked his lips with an unusually large tongue before his entire body began to twitch. His robe fell to the ground around his feet, which were no longer feet but tentacles. My eyes snapped up toward his naked body where eight, ten, fifteen, or more tentacles writhed. I gasped in horror—and maybe a little in excitement. I'd never seen an alien before. I hadn't even believed in them. Anything from space had ceased to exist in my mind or my magical realm—until now at least.

My attention stayed glued to the stage. The alien picked the elf up, suspending her in the air with his tentacles. He pinned her wrists behind her back and began to probe her. One tentacle slid over her mouth, pushing down her lower lip. She turned her head, catching it between her teeth and snarling. He shook his head, grinning with fangs longer than a vampire's. Another tentacle shot out, probing her between the legs, then another, and another. She moaned, tossing and turning in his grip.

I cocked my head to the side, trying to figure out what the hell was happening. It seemed like she had a tentacle in every hole. I didn't know much about an elf's inner workings, but either she didn't have any or he had poked holes through her heart, liver, and *spleen. At one point, I swore I'd seen the tip of a tentacle wiggle out of her ear and wave to the crowd.*

*I hadn't noticed Karen was gone until I heard a commotion coming from the bogeyman's table. I looked at her empty chair beside me before glancing as slyly as I could toward Bruno. She'd weaseled her way to him. Literally. I'd seen her perform that spell twice before. She'd turned herself into a rodent and tried to work undercover, gathering whatever information she could. But Karen's spell wasn't a match for the bogeyman and his pack. He was clutching her in his palm, and he squeezed until she fell limp, transforming back into her witchy self. The wolves dragged her out before I could catch up. I couldn't save her from her own stupid mistakes. She had known she was playing with fire.*

Thankfully, Bruno hadn't seen me with her. Or at least, if he had, he wouldn't recognize me today. Back then, I'd sported a porn 'stache and a mullet. I doubted I looked anything like my old self. I considered us safe as long as no one found out Claire was human.

I held her hand as we stepped into The Cave. The vibe felt much more different than the last time I had been here. The music echoed off the walls, and the lights still flashed, but things looked more … sinister.

"Chin up. Shoulders back. Look like a succubus. You're from the pits of hell. Remember that," I whispered, side-eyeing her and squeezing her hand in mine.

She straightened her spine and fluttered her lashes before giving me a devilish grin. My breath caught in my throat as I picked up on her emotions. She wasn't scared anymore. The energy she had bounced off of me. It was thrilling, exalting, and seductive. My dick twitched in response.

"Phew. Okay. Like that." I ran my fingers through my hair. Every tingle, every blood pump, and every feisty heartbeat that Claire gave off hit me tenfold. I'd never been in tune with anyone like this before.

I quickly pulled Claire through the crowd. No one paid us any attention or batted their eyes at us, except a group of vampires who sniffed the air when we passed. I steered her in a different direction and as far away from the vamps as possible. I didn't stop until we could no longer see a toothy fang in sight. We passed the stage where I'd watched alien porn. There weren't any exciting shows tonight—only a spiky-haired zombie on a turntable. Behind him hung a banner with the words *DJ Carl* written in blood.

"Where is he?" Claire asked, bobbing back and forth to the beats.

We mingled in a mixed crowd of gnomes, elves, and even ogres. The smell of an ogre was distinctive, atrocious, and downright gag-inducing. Surely, it could cover up any human scent clinging to Claire.

I nodded toward the table in the back. He sat in the same place, guarded by more wolves. No doubt, these wolves were much younger. Their mouths hung open, growling. Every once in a while, one would howl and set off the rest in a chorus of echoes.

"Right there. Center seat. Those men in suits with the yellow eyes are his guards—or his wolfpack."

Bruno hadn't aged a day. I'd never noticed him much when Karen was around, but now, standing even in the same room with him made me feel as small and insignificant as the gnome twerking on my shin. His broad shoulders nearly burst out of his tailored suit, which was left unbuttoned at the collar. The mythical gold chain sparkled from underneath, reflecting the flashing lights. His dark hair lay messily tousled, like he'd just come out of a hard-core romp in bed. His black eyes smoldered beneath full lashes. They smoldered! Mine only blazed.

"Wow," she said. Her tail swished behind her, slapping up against me. "I didn't think the bogeyman would look like that. I'd not be afraid for him to crawl out from under my bed. In fact, I'd welcome it. Lay out a glass of wine, light some candles, and invite that monster to eat me up."

"Okay, okay, I get it." I scowled. "He's a good-looking guy."

"He's more than good-looking! That man is straight sex. See the way his jawline—"

"Ugh," I groaned, clenching my jawline, which was apparently less stellar than Mr. Bogey-Douche's. "I'm glad you found your mate. Maybe *he* can grant you some wishes, and I'll be on my merry way then."

"Wait. Are you jealous?" She smirked, turning her back to him and her attention toward me.

I'd never been jealous before in my hundreds of years. I'd thought whatever feelings ran through me were just my reaction to hers. I'd never thought I'd experience this level of humanity. I couldn't. I was a genie. But then again, I'd not met someone like Claire before either. She hadn't been immediately impressed with me. I had to work for it with her. As much as I liked her, she was a mere human, and I was a useless genie. Besides, she was eager to get back to her world. Claire wasn't interested in anything, except my wishes.

"Huh. I guess so. I only feel you radiating a lot of pleasure from staring at him, which bounces off me and makes—oh, for fuck's sake. So, that's what jealousy feels like. I get why Karen broke Emry's bottle now. I'd probably have done worse!" My muscles flexed involuntarily beneath my shirt.

Claire laughed. "He's just a monster. You're my genie. Now, let's get that chain."

She looked up at me, fluttered her wings until she hovered inches above the ground, and planted a kiss on my cheek. I couldn't control myself. Jealousy was a fickle bitch. I put my arm around her, pulling her tight against me, and took more. She pushed her mouth harder against mine. I slipped my tongue over her lips. Her heartbeat pulsed against my chest echoing loudly against my empty chambers, as if I had a heart of my own. I felt myself throb, feeding off her vibes as I gently lowered her to the ground.

"Let's get that chain," I said.

"Yes," she breathed out, stumbling. "Chain."

I turned away, so she couldn't see my goofy grin. I'd managed to somehow sweep her off her feet without even trying.

*Eat that, Booger-Man!*

I searched for a distraction, wiggling myself free of the rascals clinging to me. One gnome in particular wouldn't stop humping my knee.

"Excuse me, sir," I asked, tapping him on his head.

"*Gobliwankinstein*," he responded, still going at it.

I sighed. I didn't speak Gnomish.

"I'm really sorry to have to do this, but you see, I'm not always a good genie. Sometimes, people rub me the wrong way. Like right now. That's my leg you're assaulting."

"*Sisoputch*." He laughed, holding on to me tighter.

I gasped. "Well, now, you've gone and done it. I was trying to be nice. But that's the tip of the iceberg. The straw that broke the camel's back. Or as I like to call it, the gnome that humped its last leg. Good day, sir." I grabbed the little man by his giant head and tossed him into the air before punting him straight toward the wolves.

They reacted as I'd expected. The werewolves ferociously broke out of their clothes, transforming into their true form, and chased after the gnome as if he were a tennis ball.

"Quick, seduce Bruno. I'm right behind you. I'll be watching. Go before those dumb dogs get back!" I pushed Claire toward the bogeyman's table.

"How the hell do I know what to say? What to do? I can't flirt! I get stupefied around hot men, if you haven't noticed."

"Are you saying I'm hot?" I wiggled my brows.

"Just forget it. I'm going. I'm going." She turned on her heels and trudged through the crowd.

I watched as she flicked her tail back and forth in front of his table. She turned to him and made eye contact before looking back toward the stage.

*Playful. She doesn't do that with me!*

His stupid, smoldering eyes fucked her before he motioned for her to join him.

She swaggered—yes, swaggered—toward him. Her breasts bounced with each step she took. I inched my way toward them, casting glances at the werewolves chasing that poor asshole gnome.

Bruno laughed, shooing his hand away toward his pack. Claire touched her collar and threw her head back in laughter too. I clenched my jaw and wondered why I hadn't just walked up to him and taken the damn chain from his neck.

The werewolves howled as the gnome escaped under a rock.

"Enough!" Bruno yelled, standing up and silencing the club. His voice carried over the music, the crowd, and his wolfpack.

The walls inside The Cave rumbled, sending bits of crumbling rock down on us. The werewolves came back with their tails tucked between their legs, and DJ Carl began to play again.

Claire reached up, patting her head, where one of her horns had suddenly disappeared. She searched the crowd until her gaze met mine, a look of horror shadowing her face. I flew by her side in a flash.

"Hello, Bruno. Pleased to meet you. I'm Dylan. I see you found my drunky friend. She has such a bad habit of wandering off when she's had too much to drink. It's the spirits that get her. Banshee water especially. Sorry if she was a bother." I cringed, hoping he would fall for the bro-code look I was giving him, letting him know this lady was batshit crazy.

Claire's wings began to sink, slowly fading into her back.

"What's that smell?" one of the bigger werewolves asked, pausing as he pulled his pants over his legs.

I always thought it must suck to have to dress and undress so much as a shifter. I only had to twirl around, and —*voilà!*—I was naked in no time.

Bruno sniffed the air.

I grabbed Claire's hand and tugged her away, apologizing. "They're only smells!" I called back, leading her away. Far, far away.

"We didn't get the chain. Magic me up again! I can do it! He liked me!"

"No. Keep walking. Toward the car. Now! Once we're out of The Cave, hang on to me. Do not let go, no matter what. Understand?" I gritted my teeth and pushed us through the crowd.

"I trust you," she said.

I believed her because I felt it. But that wasn't enough to keep Claire from fear. She felt that her life was in danger— and rightfully so. The wolves were right behind us. I could smell their bloodlust. The Karma from kicking that gnome had already caught up to me.

Claire reached behind her, feeling her back before reaching down to feel her butt.

"My tail and wings are gone! Shit." She panicked.

But the more fearful she became, the more protective I grew. We were almost to the entrance when her outfit also disappeared.

"I'm naked! I'm fucking naked! Dylan!" she cried, running.

"Lucky me! Hang on tight!" I grabbed her naked body against mine, and in a puff of smoke, I flashed us out of there.

The swamp, the thicket, and The Cave disappeared in a blur as we flew to the car. Werewolves wouldn't be able to catch me, and I was too small of a problem for Bruno to deal with. We were safe. At least, for now.

I opened the car door and stuffed Claire into the driver's seat before hopping in beside her.

"I can't drive naked. And I don't feel so good. You can't move me around like that. My body is human. I can't take it." She wobbled in her seat.

I took the key from her hand and put it in the ignition. "You'll feel better at the hotel. Just drive, and I'll put some clothes back on you. Whatever you do, don't just sit there. We have to get out of here! I don't know how to drive, or I would."

A faint howling rang out into the night, waking Claire from her trance.

"Let's get out of here!" She floored the gas pedal and took off back down the street.

We rode in silence until we reached the hotel parking lot.

"Dylan?" Her voice came out weak.

"Yes?"

"You saved me."

"I did." I patted her hand.

Her exhaustion made me uneasy.

"Dylan?" she repeated my name.

The way it hung on her lips tingled my toes.

"Um, yeah?"

"You never magicked me up some clothes," she breathed out, lazily pointing toward her body.

"Sorry. Eh, can't say that wasn't on purpose." I shrugged. My eyes followed down her beautiful curves and back up again to her halfhearted grin.

"Tsk, tsk." She let out two frail laughs before passing out and falling over onto my lap.

# CHAPTER SEVEN

CLAIRE

I YAWNED, STRETCHING MY ARMS OVER MY HEAD AND TRYING to piece together last night's events. The last thing I remembered was Dylan wrapping me in a blanket and carrying me to the room. He'd tucked me into bed with a playful flick on the nose, sending me straight into a deep sleep. I'd dreamed of Dylan and the way he had stolen that kiss in The Cave. He'd taken my breath away when he pressed his mouth on mine, stupefying me into a happy confusion. I wanted him to do it again.

"You're awake," Dylan said, startling me.

A dim glow shimmered from beneath his eyelids. He floated softly a few inches above the bed. I ran my hand down the empty sheets beneath him, wishing that he were lying next to me, touching me. The excitement from last night still coursed through my veins, and my dream lingered in my mind.

"Did I wake you?" I asked.

"No. I wasn't slumbering. I can only do that in my room.

Immortals don't sleep like humans. At least, I don't. I was just closing my eyes and thinking." He rolled over on top of me, hovering inches above my face.

"About?" I shifted under the covers, suddenly growing warm.

"About that kiss and the way your hairs stand on end when I get this close to you." He lowered himself on top of me, weightless, as if he didn't exist. "Or the way your cheeks blush when I brush my skin against yours. Or about the way you tasted when I slipped my tongue inside your mouth. I want more, and I think you do too. I heard you whisper my name in your sleep." He nuzzled his nose to mine before kissing my lips with sweet, quick pecks.

I held my breath. Each time his lips touched my skin, I felt a spark—a real spark. Not just a tingle. Dylan struck me like a match.

"Dylan, what're you doing?" I asked.

The warmth of his eyes felt like a sunburn across my cheeks.

"Shh. I'm seeing if the rest of you tastes as good as that delicious mouth of yours."

He worked his way down my body, throwing back the blanket and exposing my breasts. My nipples puckered under his breath. He took each one between his teeth and tongue, biting, licking, sucking, and playing. I arched my back and spread my legs, giving in to him. I wanted him like he'd taken me back at the nightclub—like I was his.

He nibbled my hips, working his way down to the slick spot between my legs, where I needed him to touch. I opened my legs further and further, begging him without words. His eyes snapped to mine, blazing a searing heat right through me. I felt the warmth from his gaze when he looked back down and spread me with his hand. The slight burning sensation from his flames already had me on edge.

I bucked against his face, unable to resist much longer. His tongue slid into my pussy and out again, thrusting slowly before repeatedly slipping up and over my clit.

"Oh, damn. Yes. Don't stop," I moaned.

"Is that a wish?" he mumbled.

"It's a command." I ran my hand through his hair, pushing him into me harder.

He growled, gazing up at me from between my thighs. I watched him watching me. I couldn't see his mouth, but I felt his smile. He slipped his hands under my ass and lifted me into his chin, steadily flicking my clit with his tongue. I reached beside me, grabbing the bedsheets and crumpling them in my palms. My legs began to shake as he lifted me. The entire lower half of my body was floating off the bed as he licked me into another dimension.

I threw my head back, crying out as he took me higher and higher. His fire, his touch, his tongue—all of it consumed me. I fucked his mouth, convulsing against his lips until my body shook with an orgasm that was literally not of this world. I was face-banging a genie.

Dylan flashed, dropping me back to the bed before bursting out of his shirt and pants. He climbed on top of me, his thick cock stirring against my thigh.

"I can't get pregnant or some magical STD, right? Like troll pox or fairy itch?" I asked between heavy breaths.

"No baby genies, no pox, no itch. Now, command me again. I'm all yours." He scooped me in his arms and up toward him, holding me as we hovered above the bed.

"Fuck me." I lowered my voice, wrapping my arms and legs around him. I knew he wouldn't let me fall, but sex in the air was a new experience, and gravity still played a role in my world.

He moved his hips until the tip of his cock slid straight inside of me. I quivered and let out a long moan. I hadn't realized just how much I needed him inside me until now. He pushed deep, sending us flying back against the headboard. His hand reached out, against the wall, while his other held me in a cradle, still hovering us a few feet off the bed.

I felt weightless, ethereal, excited, and needy. I wanted this man-genie. I needed this man-genie. I was going to make this man-genie mine.

I clutched his back and arched my body up while rolling him over and climbing on top. He held us suspended in the air while I slid my hips back and forth across his lap. He gripped my ass, slamming me into him faster. I squeezed my thighs, leaning forward and placing my palms on his chest. His pec muscles flexed beneath my fingertips each time I bounced.

"Hang on tight," he grunted, lifting us toward the ceiling.

The air hummed and crackled, and a flash of fire escaped from his eyes like a solar flare. He cried out, holding my hips against him while the room began to spin. I leaned down, circling my arms around his back and hanging on for dear life while his cock throbbed inside of me, filling me with a satisfying heat.

The spinning stopped, but I didn't let go. We floated back down to the bed like a feather.

"Does that make your time in the magical world a little better?" he asked, panting.

"I'd say that makes it a little more manageable. *You* make it more manageable." I laughed, leaning down and putting my head against his chest while his cock still stirred inside me. I expected to hear the racing post-orgasm *thump, thump, thump* of his pulse, but instead, I heard nothing except his heavy breaths.

"I can't hear your heart. Did I ride you so hard that it stopped? You okay?" I adjusted my head, listening to the other side of his chest.

"I don't have one," he said, gently lifting me off of him.

"What?" I sat up, covering my mouth with my hand.

"Nope. No heart."

I slumped my shoulders and turned my face from him, staring out the window. We had warmed the room so much that the glass had fogged. A low rumble of thunder rolled, drowning out the stifling silence.

"I'm feeling you again. What's wrong?" He reached for my shoulder, pulling me back into him.

"Nothing. I'm just wondering how we're going to get your spell broken without that butt plug, is all."

I pulled the blanket back over me, snuggling in next to his body, or shadow, or figure, or whatever the hell he was. He wasn't alive. No one lived without a heart. Somehow, he felt less real to me now than he had when he popped out of a dildo.

"We'll go back to Big Glug-Glug today. See what else we can find out. No worries. I'll get you your wishes, and you'll be on your way out of Morningwood soon. I promise to get you out of here. A genie's promise is binding, remember?" He stroked my hair from my face, tucking it behind my ear.

"What did you say would happen again after you grant my last wish?" I asked, laying my hand on his empty chest.

Rain pelted against the window.

"Oh. You'll just not have access to the Morningwood realm. Or any magical realms. As a human, you get one chance, and it's over. You'll be safely back into your human world and no drama from trolls, wolves, witches, me."

"No. I meant, what happens to you. Where do you go? What do you do?" I traced my fingertips across his chest and wondered if he was entirely empty inside.

"I go back into hiding ... in my dildo." He cleared his throat. "Until someone else rubs me out. Then, rinse and repeat over and over again."

"Until your flames burn out. You told me that once, but you never explained it."

He sighed, rolling over and swinging his legs off of the bed. "That's different. That's death for me. A few things can do that. My summoner can wish it. Although I've never had one who wanted to wish me dead. They're selfish enough not to use one of their wishes on me, thankfully. I've also never pissed anyone off enough, except for Karen. Course, she knew what she was doing with her curse. It's much worse than death for me. I can't fulfill my duties. My geniehood is gone."

"Jeez. I'd not wish death on anyone. Not even those wolves from last night." I shivered. "How else can your flames burn out? Asking for a friend."

"Trying to snuff me out already?" He grinned.

"Not yet." I grinned back.

"I burn out when I reincarnate into something else, like a human. Or someone plucks my eyes out and douses them in a bucket of water." He shrugged.

"Fuck. That's terrible—the last part. The human part isn't so much. How does that even happen?"

"No idea. It's not part of the genie network. No genie that has turned into a human can connect back with us and let us know. I think there's maybe a magic sword or butt plug that kills us. I hope I never find out. Either way sounds like a hell of a way to go."

My shoulders tensed. "You don't think that butt plug will kill you instead of lift the curse, right?"

"Your aunt was wicked. But she wasn't smart." He twirled into a pair of jeans and a tight-fitted tee.

"When we find this butt plug, don't touch it. I'll, um … what do I need to do with it?" I cringed, clenching my butt.

"No clue. But you're the one who said *don't touch it*. I'll let you figure that out." He raised his brows.

I shook my head and hopped out of bed, deciding to slide into a pair of jeans myself instead of having Dylan magic me up more demon lingerie. Although the sex we could have had with my wings and his tricks might have been worth it.

We dressed and readied ourselves before walking out of the hotel room together. I no longer cared about what the townspeople thought about me and my personal life. I didn't have a choice anymore. Dylan had brought me inside, wrapped in a blanket, last night. I was sure, by now, that everyone knew I hadn't spent the night alone. And hot, floaty genie sex was worth the gossip.

"Look who's growing up and not giving any fucks." He smirked, giving a halfhearted wave to the front-desk attendant.

"I'll be out of here soon enough. I'm out of fucks. Or, as we like to say where I'm from, Outer Forks!"

He reached out, pushing the lobby door open and letting me slide past him. Rain pelted down on us as we ran toward my car, quickly hopping inside.

"Outer Forks," he repeated as soon as we settled into our seats. "Tell me about it. It sounds like it must be a nice place if you're in a hurry to get back." He wiped raindrops off of his cheeks with the back of his palm.

"It's not Morningwood. That's for sure. I live in Outer Forks, but I work in Forks. The cities have different vibes. Of course, Outer Forks is much smaller. It's more hipster. Craft beer, music fests, arts festivals, and all."

I laughed, watching his brows crinkle. I had to keep reminding myself that he wasn't from my era.

"Hipster?" he asked.

"Sorry. None of this makes sense to you. You'd have to see it for yourself. You've been locked up since the '80s. I'll show you sometime." My voice caught in my throat as I realized he couldn't come with me. He'd said so himself. After my final wish, he would disappear, and I was supposed to put his dildo on a jet to France.

He turned his face away from me and stared out the window.

I slumped forward in my seat, letting the air hit the back of my damp shirt. The thick drizzle pelted down on my car, skewing everything in front of me into a white blur. I clutched the steering wheel and craned my neck forward, struggling to see the road ahead.

"Weren't you supposed to call your mom and let her know we're coming?" he asked, breaking the silence.

"It's a weekday. She's working. Besides, we're only trying to pry more information out of Big Glug-Glug. We won't be there long at all." I slammed on my brakes, nearly missing our turn.

"This time, you hold on tight." I nudged him with my elbow, trying to lighten the heavy tension in the air.

He blew out a breath through his nose but said nothing. I couldn't get a laugh or a smile.

"I think I'm vibing off you now. What's up?" The familiar crunching of the gravel road as we drove toward my mom's place sent a shiver up my spine.

"Ah, nothing. I'm just thinking about the butt plug. Heh."

"Look, I've lived through a very depressing childhood. My mom was an alcoholic, and my aunt abused me. I had zero friends in this hellhole of a town. I lived for years, escaping with my nose between the pages of fairy tales, only to wake up and find out my life was a nightmare. So, I know sadness when I see it. And I definitely know it when I feel it. Tell me what's got you down." I pulled up to the front of the old house right as a bolt of lightning crashed overhead.

"Ominous. Cliché," I muttered.

"Is this sadness? I've been lonely before but not sad. Not like this anyway. It feels ... my chest feels empty, which is weird because it is empty. I feel like there's a gaping hole in it. I'm not sure why." He put his hand between his pecs, right where his heart should be.

"You're heartbroken. You're picking it up from me. I'm sorry. It's because I thought about not being able to show you my place. I mean, I can. Maybe you can just grant me the wishes afterward? Or—"

He cleared his throat. "I'm not heartbroken. That's impossible. I'm a genie, and I have a job to do. You're getting your wishes. Hopefully today." He opened the car door and stepped into a low-lying fog.

"What's this? I've never seen anything like it." I pushed myself up and out of the car, motioning toward the thick vapors rolling out of the surrounding woods. "Is something else here besides Big Glug-Glug? Did those wolves find out where we are? I swear, if small-town gossip gets me killed, I'll—" I started.

Dylan appeared by my side in a flash. He swung his arms around my waist, holding me tight against him.

The rain drizzled into a fine mist.

"Shh. Whatever it is, it isn't good. It's not the wolves though. They can't do this. They'd only rip us apart like a chew toy. This is something different. Like someone's playing a trick." He gestured at the curls of vapor climbing up our legs.

I shivered against his chest, wishing I could hear the comforting *thump, thump, thump* of a heart he didn't have.

Another bolt of lightning snapped through the air, crackling overhead.

"Let's get inside and get this over with." I tried to make my way toward the front door, but my feet wouldn't budge. They felt like cement boots under the fog. I grunted, pulling my shoe out of the dense vapors and freeing my foot. "I think we're in a trap," I said, freeing my other foot.

A glowing emerald light fluttered above, hissing in Dylan's face.

Dylan s eyes flashed as he turned his head toward the sky and roared. The hairs on the back of my neck prickled. I took a step back, lost my footing, and fell to the ground. The fog quickly circled me, curling its sticky tendrils around my throat. I tried to scream, but it choked me into silence.

# CHAPTER EIGHT

DYLAN

THE MOMENT I SAW EMRY FLUTTERING ABOUT, I KNEW THINGS were about to get crazy. Green faeries were only around when trouble was around, and this green faerie in particular had caused enough pain for me.

"Time to go!" I picked Claire up, threw her over my shoulder, and ran to the porch.

The tendrils of fog grabbed at my ankles in a slimy, wet death trap, tripping me twice before I made it to the front door. I didn't have time to waste, looking for a key. I kicked in the door and slammed it shut behind me, barring it with a couch, three chairs, and a TV.

"What just happened?" Claire's voice quivered. Her hand rubbed the scorched marks on her throat. "Was that green light a faerie? Was that Emry?"

I sat on the couch and exhaled. "Yep. I have no idea where she came from, but since she's here, that means trouble. I guess this house must have a spell on it. I wonder why it's going off now. We must be close to solving this butt-plug quest." I held out my hands for her to join me on the couch. "Come here. Let me see that. Are you okay?"

She sat down next to me, still profusely rubbing at her throat. I brushed her hair behind her shoulders and inspected the red welts roping around her neck.

"It burns. But not like a regular burn. It's cold. Like eating too much mint." She pressed her fingertips on a dark purple spot at the nape of her neck and flinched.

"Try not to touch it. We'll have to deal with it back at the hotel. We can't stay here. Let's figure out how to get back to the car. I can probably distract that fog, and you can run."

She squinted her eyes, wincing. I felt her pain. It whipped through me, burning me up from the inside out. I curled my fists, letting out a staggered breath.

"Let's just get what we came here for and be done with it. You lost your geniehood to that bitch Karen! I'm not going to sit back and let her keep pushing you, me, or anyone else around. Even in her death, she's hurting us. This has to stop. And it starts with that damn butt plug! My first wish is to fix all the wrongs she's done to everyone, starting with you. Now, let's go to Big Glug-Glug and fix this shit. It'll all be over soon." She stood up, shivering and tugging at my arm.

"Now, who's saving who?" I smiled, pulling her down to my lap. "You know no one's ever been concerned with my geniehood or my life. Or lack thereof. I've sat in that lonely dildo for ages. Before you came along, things were beginning to get to me. I'd have even taken a ride in an ogre's butt, just to come out into the world again. But you … you're so much better than an ogre's asshole. I know I don't have a heart, so maybe I'm playing off your emotions, but the way you make me feel is so human. And I like it. And you. I like you. I know we're on different realms and that this couldn't—"

*Crash. Bang. Pop.*

A commotion came from the attic, jolting us both upright.

I put my finger to my lips, shushing Claire while I listened. The house was silent.

She put her nose in the air and sniffed, recoiling. I, too, noticed a familiar scent.

"You said I'm safe with you. I still am, right? I saw you set that whole swamp up in burning blue flames. You can get us out of here. I know you can. But ... I'm running down to the basement. Cliché, I know. Dumb lady runs straight into trouble." She put her hands up in protest as I tried to stop her from running off. "You can come with me down there, or you can stay up here. But I'm ending this right here and right now. Just have my back. Use your fiery mumbo jumbo."

She ran off in the direction of the basement. I followed on her heels, stepping over piles of trash, blankets, and pillows. Her mom had left this place worse than the last time we'd been here. Boxes of rat poison lay strewn about amid the empty beer cans.

We entered the kitchen as soon as the lights began to flicker. The storm outside surged, whipping tree branches across the windows like fingernails on a chalkboard.

Again, the familiar scent filled the air. I reached out, clasping her sweaty palm.

"What is it?"

"I'm sorry, Claire. It's not safe. I'm getting you out of here. I don't think I'll ever be able to give you those wishes. We need to get out now! She's here. I can handle many things, but she has me by the balls—er, butt plug. I'd not forgive myself if anything happened to you. Your life is more important than my geniehood."

I grabbed her, sweeping her off her feet. She squirmed in my arms.

"Put me down! I can do this! I've read fairy tales! The

good guys win! Just let me try. I need those wishes!" She bucked against me, growling.

I'd felt this vibe countless times—greed. No matter how many wishes I granted, my summoners always wanted more. It was a good thing I disappeared after their last wish. Otherwise, they might extinguish my fire out of frustration.

"You're not thinking clearly. No wish is so important that it endangers your life." I held her tight against me and ran for the front door.

A cackle rang out, filling the room with a burst of evil laughter that cut through me like a knife. Claire's face dropped as she quit struggling in my arms.

"Is she a ghost? Great Aunt Karen is dead. She can't be here." Her voice shook as I opened up the door. It slammed itself shut, the bolts automatically locking.

"Fuck!" I set Claire down.

I turned in circles, searching for an escape, but each doorway shimmered in a black veil I was familiar with. Only death awaited on the other side of those things. I'd seen it once before long ago, during my second summons. I'd worked for a vampire then, who had fallen in love with a witch. They'd both crossed the black veil together as their last wish. I never mentioned it to Claire or anyone. Their death would weigh on my conscience for eternity. But I couldn't have stopped them.

*Cackle, cackle, cackle.*

*Pop. Flash. Bang.*

Karen appeared in a cloud of smoke, wearing a typical black witch's robe.

*Cliché,* as Claire would say.

Karen's skin hung off of her in wrinkled gray flaps. Her lips were nothing but a pencil-thin line, as if someone had drawn a snarl across her face. I'd never seen anything so old in my life.

"No, I'm not a ghost! Do you think I'd be caught dead as a ghost? Get it? Dead as a ghost?" Karen cackled. "Especially after all that ghosting this son of a bitch did to me, I don't like ghosts much. But I don't like genies more. Or you, dear. You always thought you were so smart with your little books and journals. Putting your nose in the air anytime you came around."

I shoved Claire behind me, holding out my arms to cover her. I felt her fear through her rapid pulse pressed against my back.

"Oh. Well, look at that. So, you two are a thing." Karen's decrepit face sagged so low that I thought her chin would fall off.

"You're such a bitch! Do you know that? You aren't a witch. You're a smelly, rotten, old, ugly hag of a bitch. I am so sick of your shit. You were the worst when I was growing up, and you're still the worst now. Going around, treating others like shit to make yourself feel better. Karen!" Claire shoved my arm aside, stepping in front of me.

Her quickening pulse wasn't fear. It was adrenaline. I wondered if, when I'd magicked her wings, I'd also somehow magicked her a backbone.

"Watch who you're talking to. I've got what you want. One more word out of you, and—*poof!*—it's gone. Your lover boy here will forever be useless to you. And you'll become more and more frustrated as the greed takes you over."

Claire looked up at me, creasing her brows.

"She's—" I started.

"Oh, ho, ho! He didn't tell you that, did he? He only told you the good things. He can do this and that. Well, he can also make you miserable. Ahem, look at me. I hide in varmints, hopping from rat to weasel to rodent to stay alive so that I can prevent him from ever being truly happy again. Shame, shame. Shouldn't have crossed me, Dylan."

*Cackle, cackle, cackle.*

"Wha's she talking about?" Claire took a step away from me.

"It's nothing. I was trying to get this all sorted before that happened."

"Lies. Such a liar. Did you think you'd get it sorted and be a match for me? Ha! Over my not-so-dead body!" Karen said. Her arm twitched and fell to the ground.

"You can't even keep yourself together. How old are you now? A hundred and twenty? You look like death! Go crawl back into a rat and get your energy back. Otherwise, yeah, you'll have to become a match for me. I've only grown stronger. You? You're dying."

Karen grunted, picking her arm up and shoving it back into her shoulder.

"Lying about what, Dylan? Tell me." Claire began to rub the wounds on her neck again.

"As long as he's out, you're going to get greedy. It'll get worse and worse until it consumes you." Karen grinned.

"Is that true, Dylan? Is that why I wanted to go down to the basement, knowing it was dangerous? Why didn't you tell me it was going to do this to me? I don't want to become obsessed or greedy or anything like that." Claire backed away from me.

"Oh, you will. You'll both become miserable, and there's nothing you can do about it because I got this!" Karen cackled again, turning around and lifting her robes. Her ass drooped, melting down her legs like a deflated balloon. She bent over, pantyless, exposing a blue butt plug, complete with a witch hat handle on the end.

"You always did have a stick up your ass, Karen." I cringed.

Claire gasped, covering her eyes.

Karen let her robe fall back to her feet and turned back toward us.

"Still the comedian. Let's see if you think it's funny when I do this." Karen twirled her fingers in the air, sending tendrils of vapor at Claire's throat again.

Claire grabbed her throat and began gagging.

"Stop! She's gagged enough, seeing your disgusting, wrinkled, old balloon knot. Leave her alone. It's me you want. I saw Emry floating about too. Why don't you punish us both? Claire never did anything to you. You're only jealous of her. Enough!" I roared, sending a ball of fire directly into Karen's chest and knocking her over.

She lay on the floor, coughing up plumes of black smoke. Claire heaved beside me, catching her breath. The vapor vanished.

"You're too old. Give me the butt plug, and we're leaving. It's done." I stepped toward her, prepared to take it from her myself.

"You'll never catch me," Karen said.

A loud pop rang out through the room as she transformed into a gopher.

"Mom was right!" Claire pointed at the rodent as it scurried toward the front door. "Great Aunt Karen *is* the gopher!"

"What the fuck is all of this commotion going on here? I'm trying to get my beats down, and all I hear is a bunch of snap, cracklin', and poppin'!" Big Glug-Glug appeared, dragging his swollen belly across the black veil.

I'd always heard goblins were immune to the veil of death, but I never believed it myself.

Karen, the gopher, squealed, raking her claws across the wooden floors.

"Ah, hell. You didn't have to bring me lunch." Big Glug-Glug unhinged his jaw and stuck out his snakelike tongue, catching Karen by the tail and dropping her in his mouth before I could stop him.

"Wait! My butt plug!" I yelled, clutching my eyes. They began burning as if someone had thrown acid on them—goblin stomach acid. My life was bound to that sex toy stewing in Big Glug-Glug's gut.

Claire screamed, grabbing on to me as I fell back, hitting my head against the floor.

"Your eyes! Dylan, they're fading. You're flickering out. Help him!" she shouted at the goblin.

"What'd I do?" He turned his fat head left and right, confused.

"You ate the butt plug. He needs it! If you want that fucking gold chain, cough it up! Now. I'll use my wish for your chain, just give me the butt plug! He's dying!" she screamed through sobs.

Claire's voice wavered in and out, in sync with my flickering body. I began to fade like a low signal on the genie network. The pain in my eyes seared through me in a scorching heat that made me wish for death. I tried to apologize to Claire. I'd never felt more real or more alive than I had these past few days with her. But I choked on my breath, waving her away. It was pointless now. I was too far gone.

# CHAPTER NINE

CLAIRE

I COULDN'T MAKE SENSE OF WHAT WAS HAPPENING. MY HUMAN brain didn't function in this realm as it did in reality. One second, my great aunt had been back, and the next, she was dead again, eaten alive by a fat, rapping goblin.

From the corner of my eye, I saw Dylan lying on the floor, writhing. His head tossed and turned as he clutched his eyes like he wanted to claw them out.

"Hang in there!" I screamed at him before turning my attention to the goblin. "I'll cut you open and fish that butt plug out myself if you don't cough up that gopher's asshole this instant!" I lunged toward Big Glug-Glug.

He yelped, rolled back, lifted a leg, and farted out the butt plug. It lay mangled in a puddle of goo. Or poo. Whatever the fuck goblins sharted out from the pits of hell that were their stomachs.

"Sorry. It's all that's left. Everything else is gone. Doctors give me antacids, but they don't help." He belched loudly.

"Dylan! Dylan! I have it!" I reached for the mangled toy,

grabbing it in horror. I choked back a gag and waved it in front of his face.

His body lay still, limp, and lifeless. His eyes were nothing but a faint glimmer, flickering like a candle in its last moments. I sat up, afraid to breathe. One soft breath, and I could blow those flames out forever.

"Dylan? I got the butt plug. You can be free now. We can be free. Together? What do I do? Please. Can you hear me? What do I do?" I sat beside him, rubbing his arms as if I could wake him up.

He didn't flinch.

"Stay with me! I wish you'd just stay with me. Don't leave me alone. Please, don't go. I don't have anyone else," I cried.

He didn't answer.

"Dylan! Dylan! Wake up! Please! Stay with me," I whispered again to flames that had already died. I stared into his black eyes and saw my dark reflection. I knew I'd never see myself blazing in his gaze again.

I closed my eyes and took a deep breath. When I opened them again, everything was gone and back to normal. The butt plug had disappeared, the death fog had disappeared, the burning wounds around my neck had disappeared, and even that disgusting goblin wasn't anywhere to be found.

I picked myself up from the floor and drove back to the hotel, delirious with an ache that gnawed through my chest. I'd never had anyone like Dylan in my life before. I had no friends or family other than my unreliable mother. My ex-lovers had never stuck around for more than a few weeks. In the short amount of time I'd known Dylan, he'd shown me kindness, laughter, passion. He'd shown me the world, both mine and his. Now, I was alone again.

I burst through the door of my hotel room and frantically searched for the dildo. I thought that maybe, just maybe, he'd magicked himself back into it. But the toy had vanished too. I let out a wail and face-dived into my bed, sobbing. I clutched the blanket to me, breathing in his smoky scent that still lingered in the sheets. I had nothing of Morningwood left. It was gone, and he was gone too.

Dylan had said he would free me from this fantasyland and that it would be over soon. He had known I struggled with living in his world. He'd promised to end it for me, and he had. A genie's promise was binding.

TWO WEEKS LATER

I sat at my desk, tapping my pen on a blank page.

Last week, I'd nailed the article on Morningwood. I'd written a tale of ghosts, witches, and even goblins. I'd spun a fictional story littered with historical facts, and our readers ate it up. I'd also mentioned Fat Sal, who, last I'd heard, had bought yet another car to add to her fleet of rentals. I didn't say anything about Great Aunt Karen. The last thing I wanted to do was glorify that old hag.

"Got another one of those wild tales of yours? I think you need to do a piece on the rivalries at FU Fashion Academy. You can spin that into something crazy. Maybe the bully stuff that seems to be all the rage," my boss said, stopping at my desk.

"Hmm. There's an idea. I'll look into it. Thanks." I glanced at the clock on the wall.

It was already time for me to leave, and I hadn't even written a single word today. Or yesterday. Or the day before.

I'd poured my heart and soul into the tale of Morning-wood as soon as I arrived back home. I never mentioned Dylan. I couldn't speak his name aloud or write it or even think about it without becoming a sobbing mess.

I packed my bags and left the night he died. I ghosted Morningwood and everyone in it. I couldn't even bring myself to call my mother, and she never called to check on me either.

I took my notebook and laptop and left for home in silence—my new normal. I drove in silence and made dinner in silence. I dressed for bed in silence and lay for hours in silence. I had no one to talk to and nothing to say. The silence was comforting for me because, in those quiet moments, I was able to remember. I remembered the wacky way Dylan had emerged from his magic dildo and how he'd tapped my nose and sent me into a peaceful sleep. I remembered the heat I'd felt as he made love to me, spinning us in the air in a whirlwind of lust, and the way my skin had sparked against his touch.

But most of all, I sat quietly in silence so that I could concentrate on remembering the fire in his eyes. I felt his piercing gaze like a flaming arrow to my soul. I still felt it if I sat motionless, focusing long enough on my memories. My body warmed at the thought, as if he were touching me all over again.

I lay back on my bed and stared up at the ceiling, crying again. I'd never known how lonely I was until I lost Dylan. I'd managed to live a simple life just fine. I had been happy with my books and my work. I'd shut out my mom and Morningwood for years, and I didn't feel bad about it. I was happier on my own. There was less drama that way.

Unlike my fairy tales, I didn't need a prince to save me. I'd chosen to save myself when I decided to leave that place —twice.

But now, I wished someone would save me. I wished I had a mom that I could call up and cry to, or a best friend to come over and listen, or a genie to hold me one last time.

*Knock. Knock. Knock.*

I sat up, startled. No one ever came to my house, except delivery drivers and the mailman. I didn't think I had any packages coming, and I surely hadn't ordered a pizza. I grabbed a tissue and dried my face.

*Knock. Knock. Knock.*

I tiptoed to the door and peeked out the peephole. A big, dark eye stared back at me.

"Ah!" I screamed, jumping back.

"Claire?" a familiar voice asked.

I grabbed the knife I kept on the entry table and opened the door, ready to strike in case Great Aunt Karen was sending me tricks from her grave.

"Finally! Do you have any idea how many Claire Jacksons there are in Outer Forks? Jeez! I've been looking for you all over the place!" Dylan threw his hands in the air.

"Dylan?" I dropped the knife and stepped into him, touching his face, his arms, his chest. "This can't be right. You're not real. Your eyes aren't blazing. Besides, I saw you vanish. You burned out."

"I'll pretend I didn't see that weapon." He swatted my hands away. "I'm real. You wished for it."

"I did?"

"Yeah. You clutched the butt plug in your hand and said, 'Stay with me! I wish you'd just with me,' " he mocked me in a girlish voice before clearing his throat. "Turns out, that's what saved my soul when I was being burned from the inside out through a cursed magic butt plug dissolving in a pit of goblin goo." He shivered. "Bet you never thought you'd hear that sentence."

"I don't understand. I thought Morningwood and your realm was closed off to me now."

"It is. I'm not a genie anymore. I'm human. Feel." He took my palm in his, placing it on his chest.

"You have a heart!" I jumped up on my heels. "I feel it! You have a heart." I laughed, falling into his chest. I turned my cheek against his heartbeat and closed my eyes, letting the *thump, thump, thump* of his heart sync with mine.

He put his arms around me. "It's all because of you. You used your wish on me. Now, it all makes sense. When my other genie friends burned out, I guess they all went to their human form, unable to communicate back about what had done it. I guess they had friends and lovers wish for them too. Who knows? I might have vanished from the magical Morningwood realm, but I turned back up at the hotel for some odd reason. Maybe because that was where my dildo was. I stashed it under the mattress in case those gossipy maids decided to snoop."

"Is that where it was? I went back and looked for it before I left. But I never thought to look under the mattress. I assumed it'd vanished with you."

"You must have gotten out of town fast! When I popped back up at the hotel, you were already gone. It was still nighttime. Not sure how much time had passed before I reappeared again though. I've been hiding out on the streets and slowly making my way to Outer Forks ever since.

"Some nice women from a pink taco truck helped me out. They fed me and gave me some clothes. One of them— her name was Nikki—said she knew I wasn't from this world. I'm not sure how she knew that, but she believed me and my story. She helped me track you down. So, here I am."

"I can't believe you're real. I've spent the last two weeks thinking I killed you. I shouldn't have made us go back into that house!" I wiped a tear from my cheek.

He kissed the top of my forehead and held me out at arm's length. "It was the greed eating at you. You weren't thinking straight. I should have warned you about that. I'm so sorry. I thought I could fix things before that settled in. I was wrong. You didn't kill me. You saved me. You gave me a heart." He tapped his chest.

"But your flames are gone." I searched his eyes for a sign of myself blazing back but only saw my regular, dark reflection.

"Pfft. Who needs fiery eyes when I can now eat Mack Daddies without feeling like shit? Besides, I think I can still do a smoldering stare. How's this?" He squinted his eyes and wiggled his brows like he was fighting some weird kind of face spasm.

"Yeah, how about you not do that? We can work on it. I'll teach you some human things. You have so much to learn!" I laughed, pulling him inside.

"I never did get that smolder down. Hey, do you think we can grab one of those craft beers you were talking about too? And maybe we can get a hipster." He kicked the door shut behind him.

"Get a hipster?" I tugged him toward my bedroom.

"Yeah. You said you have hipsters here. I'm assuming that's like a fanny pack. I need something to stash this in. For memory's sake." He pulled out his old blue dildo from inside his pants and waved it in front of my face.

"A hipster is a person! Not a purse. Jeez! Have you been walking around with a plastic dildo in your pants? I thought you were just happy to see me." I paused, pulling him into me and double-checking his heartbeat again.

*Thump, thump, thump.*

"Thrilled to see you, darling. Thrilled." He picked me up off my feet, cradling me in his arms.

For a moment, I felt like we were floating again.

# EPILOGUE

**CLAIRE**

I sat in my home office, admiring the growing stack of fairy tales and paranormal books I'd written.

Over the years, I'd made a career change, thanks to Dylan's support. It was a struggle at first for both of us, financially and emotionally. Getting him used to the human world and conditioned for a job was more work than I'd imagined.

Eventually, things fell into place, and he found his calling as a stand-up comedian at the local nightclubs. He'd brought in so many crowds that he had become a regular celebrity at a popular bar called The Lounge. On nights I couldn't attend his gigs, I'd sit at home in silence again. It wasn't the same sad silence I'd put myself through those hellish weeks he'd been away from me. My new silence was comfortable, peaceful, and allowed me to reflect on my journey and how far we'd come.

*My name is Fritzi Cox, and this is my fairy tale*, I typed on my laptop.

"Ah, are you writing our story? With your pen name? What're you going to call it? *Fritzi and The Magic Dildo?*" Dylan peered over my shoulders and rubbed the back of my neck.

"Ha! That title would sure draw attention. I think it's time for me to write about us. I need to get it out. Before this little one gets out." I patted my swollen belly. "You know, this will require a trip back to Karen's place for some research. Mom said she cleaned it up—along with herself."

"It's because all of the bad energy left. Karen's wicked bullshit probably made your mom's problems ten times worse. Now that Karen's out of there, she's slowly healing. As much as she can anyway."

I hoped he was right, but I'd been through these phases all my life with my mother, and one thing was sure—she never changed.

"Do you think Big Glug-Glug is still there? Maybe he's a best-selling rap artist now, playing at The Cave for Bruno and the wolves. Gosh, that sounds like a band name. If only my readers knew how real my books were!" I laughed.

"They're probably like you. Wishing for their fairy tales and not realizing just how batshit crazy fantasy realms really are." He leaned down, nuzzling my cheek.

"I'm still living my fairy tale even if, sometimes, it does get batshit crazy." I sighed, turning my head to meet his lips.

"Oh!" I flinched, rubbing the top of my belly. "He's been giving me the worst heartburn. I wonder where he gets that from."

"Beats me. I've not been fiery for years! Are you sure you haven't been sneaking around with some other genie?" he teased, hoisting me out of my chair and into his arms—my favorite place.

*Thump, thump, thump.*

"Well, there was this one time I rubbed a vibrator," I said, nuzzling my head into his chest.

"Who s the comedian now?" He laughed.

"So, when I get mad, instead of sending you to the doghouse, I'll send you back to your dildo," I said, smirking.

"Whoa! You got jokes! Is this a side effect of pregnancy? Are you roasting me? How cliché! I'm rubbing off on you."

He stared down at me. For a fleeting moment, I swore I could see my reflection blazing back.

"Ba-dum-cha!" I smiled, tapping his nose.

Thank you so much for reading Ghosted! I hope you enjoyed my dive into the paranormal world. If you'd like to stay in Morningwood and party with vampires, click below to begin Fritzi Ccx's VILF series.

*One-Click Royally Drained today!*

Signup for my NEWSLETTER to find more information on my latest releases, and claim your exclusive, free ebook!

**https://kataddams.com/free-book**

Join my Facebook group, D.T.F. (Dirty. Tough. Females), for news, sneak-peeks, and more!

# ALSO BY KAT ADDAMS

**Dirty South Series**

*Faking Second Chances*

*Schooling Professor Playboy*

*Playing Backstage with the Rockstar*

*Stroking the Boss's ... Ego*

*Mayday (FREE for Newsletter Subscribers)*

**DTF (Dirty. Tough. Female.) Series**

*On the Rox*

*Cream-Pied*

*Whip it Out*

*Just the Tip*

**FU (FORKS UNIVERSITY FASHION ACADEMY) SERIES**

*Just Between Us*

*This Means War*

**BUCK OFF RANCH SERIES**

*Josie Thatcher, Cowboy Catcher*

*Emma Jean, Heartbreak Queen*

**PARANORMAL ROMANTIC COMEDY**

*Ghosted*

**WRITING PARANORMAL ROMANTIC COMEDY AS FRITZI COX**

*Royally Drained*

*Royally Cursed*

*Royally Revamped*

*Home Sweet Home*

*Toxic Chemistry*

**For a complete listing of Kat Addams books, visit**

https://kataddams.com

# ACKNOWLEDGMENTS

As always, thank you to my daughter. Your imagination inspires me to embrace the wackiness and stay true to myself. I love you! You're not allowed to read my books until you're forty.

Thank you to my amazing editor, Jovana Shirley, who makes my books shine. I would be so lost without you! Also, thanks to my amazing cover designer, Lori Jackson, who also makes my books sparkle. You two are the most amazing team I could ask for in this business.

Also, thank you to Dani Smith and Alex Julian, for lending me your talent. Your art is amazing, and you always put my ideas to paper perfectly. You're so much fun to work with too!

Thank you to Kari, my assistant, who takes care of pretty much everything so I can keep writing. You've been the biggest help to me, and I appreciate you so much. You are an awesome person to work with, and I'm so grateful we connected!

Thank you to the bookstagrammers, the readers, my ARC team, and DTF for supporting me and sharing my work. Your enthusiasm keeps me going. I wouldn't thrive without all of you.

And lastly, thank you to my own Big D for encouraging me and never letting me quit, even on those super-tough days. You always pick me up and push me forward. You've been the support I needed in my life. If I could rub a magic dildo, I'd wish for you on the other side. And maybe that place in Jackson Hole too. I love you.

# ABOUT THE AUTHOR

Kat Addams is an author of contemporary romantic comedies. She's had a passion for making readers laugh since she wrote her first over-the-top comic book at the age of eight, earning her high marks and concerning looks from her grade-school teachers. She's a graduate of the University of Memphis, where she studied English literature and creative writing, and fell in love with the rom-com genre. Her books can be described as equal parts shameless and heartwarming with a heavy dose of heat.

When she's not writing about exotic men and daydreaming of worldly travels, you can find Kat in her hometown of Memphis, drinking craft cocktails on patios and raising her mini-me with a girl-power attitude—but not necessarily in that order. In her downtime, she loves to embark on outdoor adventures, empower other women, and lose herself in good books and good music.

Kat satisfies her darker side by writing paranormal romance with wicked humor under the name Fritzi Cox. Fritzi provides Kat with an outlet to cause mayhem and debauchery with an element of suspense. Whether you're reading a book from either Fritzi or Kat, you're guaranteed a hilarious adventure.